ALL THAT GLITTERS

A HOUSE SECRETS NOVELLA

Imogene Nix

Secrets World introduction

As the Danu's Secrets is a continuation of the Blood Secrets & House Secrets trilogies, some readers may come into the series, unknowing of what has gone before. I've added the blurbs for all the Blood Secrets and House Secrets books to assist you to understand the world you are entering. I have also added the blurb for All that Glitters which is a crossover novella between the House Secrets and Danu's Secrets stories.

The Blood Bride Blurb:

Hope just wants to be an ordinary nestling. She went to college and escaped, but now she's back and there's a secret everyone is keeping from her.

Xavier is the new master of the nest, ready to welcome home the daughter of the house who he has never met. He's unprepared for the woman who steals his breath and enchants him.

Now Hope and Xavier must fight for lives and those of the innocents. After all, it is only by overcoming the rogues that they will have a chance of a timeless future together. But will it be in time?

Warning: If you love sexy alpha males that go bump

in the night, hot and heavy encounters and strong females, then this book is for you...

The Illuminated Witch Blurb

After years of struggling alone, Celina – a witchling of immense power – must find her place in the world of vampires.

Javed is building a new nest – the first new one in a century – and struggling to overcome his own demons, as an ancient evil stirs.

With Celina in danger, the demands of a fledgling nest and time running out, what are the chances their love can overcome every obstacle?

The Sorcerer's Touch Blurb:

Since the Slaughterhouse Rout, Daniel has nursed his abilities, but the decision he faces will change his life and those of everyone around him.

Whether the change is positive or not remains to be seen.

Cressida fears that history will repeat itself. Once before she lost everything she held dear, but after centuries of hiding she must face her past in order to

forge a new future. Has she waited too long and pushed Daniel away too well?

The darkness draws closer...

Just as the House Secrets book follow the original Blood Secrets series, so do the Danu's Secrets. However, below is a small taste of the House Secrets Trilogy (however Danu's Secret book 1, takes place after House Secrets Book 2.) As Dawn Breaks takes place at the same time as *Blood Secrets* "The Sorcerer's Touch," and is essentially a *continuation* of the Blood Secrets trilogy. To know how the Blood Secrets storyline ends, you do need to read The Sorcerer's Touch.

While the books **can** be read on its own, you have a better understanding of the world by reading the books which precede this one.

In As Dawn Breaks, we finally learn about David and his happy ending.

As Dawn Breaks Blurb:

Genevieve is many things, but no single title fits her quite as accurately as '*mutt*'—the one bestowed by her vicious ex-boyfriend. She's built a life, far from the family who've disowned her—one she's proud of—as a police officer with the Paranormal Liaison Division, and hiding from the world.

David is brittle from his experiences with his ex-wife Alexa, the truth his parents duped him his whole life, and he's trying to come to terms with the fallout of those beliefs, running a nest and feeling like an imposter.

A chance meeting between Genevieve and David opens up an opportunity for hope amid the grim realities of paranormal warfare.

Trusting each other may be their only choice, but the past always bites back and this time is no different.

HOUSE
SECRETS

how many secrets are hidden from view?

All That Glitters Blurb:

Genny and David had a wild and tumultuous romance, but now the were-pair must travel to Ireland where Genny will undertake her initial education as a leprechaun-were hybrid quickly.

As with all best intentions, things don't go as planned.

Padraic—Genny's father—is placing a wedge between them, and David is spectacularly unhappy with the growing distance between the pair. He just needs her back where she belongs... in his arms.

Genny doesn't see the danger at first, not until the night David doesn't come to her bed, then realisation hits, but with demons and secrets, demanding goddesses and lore all clashing, the two must work together as a couple.

They both know the only way to achieve that is with willpower and love.

All That Glitters

Genny and David had a wild and tumultuous romance, but now the were-pair must travel to Ireland where Genny will undertake her initial education as a leprechaun-were hybrid quickly.

As with all best intentions, things don't go as planned.

Padraic—Genny's father—is placing a wedge between them, and David is spectacularly unhappy with the growing distance between the pair. He just needs her back where she belongs... in his arms.

Genny doesn't see the danger at first, not until the night David doesn't come to her bed, then realisation hits, but with demons and secrets, demanding goddesses and lore all clashing, the two must work together as a couple.

They both know the only way to achieve that is with willpower and love.

Note:

This book is a Secrets World Novel and can be read stand alone, but for the best experience, you should read As Dawn Breaks beforehand.

Foreward and US/UK Disclaimer

All That Glitters, is a crossover between the House Secrets series and Danu's Secrets. As such it can be read alone, but is best after completing the Blood Secrets trilogy and the first book of the House Secrets trilogy, as that is chronologically where it takes place.

Please note also:

The UK and USA share the English language, but there are many words that are spelled differently. Some words have extra letters in the British spelling, such as the word cancelled. In American English, it is spelled canceled. There also words that interchange the letters c or s and sometimes z. For example, in America, you spell offense and in Britain, it is written as offence. We also use the letter u in many words, such as colour and flavour.

These spellings are **not** incorrect.

This book is written in UK English to reflect my Australian/English background.

Ebook: 978-1-922369-59-8

Paperback: 978-1-922369-60-4

Editing by Pamela Tyler

Cover by Dexpress Covers

January 2023
Well, here I am back at my computer finalising the files for All That
Glitters, and one of the last tasks is writing this dedication.
I always find this difficult, because, where do you start?
So in no particular order, I need to thank my cover designer, Jocelyn
and my editor, Pamela. There's my crew of dedicated supporters
especially Keri and Suzi.
My family, Mark, Charlotte and of course now introducing Nathan,
along with Kaylah and Winston—my super trusty buddies at home.
Thank you to my Imogene Nix's Makers and Fakers - love you all lots!
I know I've missed people, and for those I have, apologies.
Hugs to you all!
Imogene

Chapter One

Genevieve sighed and slipped off her shoes, padding from the doorway into the kitchen. The house was empty, and for a moment, she closed her eyes. Let her mind wander back to the period when she'd she lived by herself, in total isolation from anyone else. She'd not really been content. Hell, she'd barely been surviving.

David had changed all that for her.

He'd changed her.

The sound of a vehicle approaching in the distance had her turning. She knew the vehicle, the sound of the engine. *David.*

She'd offered to cook tonight, and the steak in the bag sitting on the bench called, the scent of meat and blood intoxicating. She sniffed and smiled. "Better get it on," she muttered.

With deft moves, she tugged the small pack of steak from the bag and grabbed a knob of butter to drop into the pan. The vegetable she craved—green, who would have thought it—sat in their own packet. This was a new choice of accompaniment. Yet another David influence.

By the time the meat was sizzling, the door opened and in walked

David. Her partner and mate. As always, she took a moment to gaze at him below her eyelashes, while her body reacted instinctively to his proximity, breasts tingling along with other body parts.

"My lovely wife-to-be." He gathered her close, and the kiss was hot as mouths melded together.

She stretched up, looping her arms around his neck, and when he ended the kiss, she was grateful for the support. "Well, I do like that kind of welcome."

He grinned. "So much the better, because we're alone." David cupped her cheek with a gentle hand. "How was your day?"

When Genevieve glanced down, he frowned. "It was awful, David. I mean, the fallout from Julien—"

"That bastard," muttered David.

"Bastard or not, he's left us a colossal mess." Her ex-partner and one-time lover had double-crossed everyone. He'd pulled off multiple murders while pretending to be a range of professionals, including a realtor. He'd further added insult to injury with a letter egging them to track him down. "Simon's still on the warpath about Niamh's situation—"

"She's recovering?"

Genevieve nodded at his query. "Physically, yes. But emotionally, it's going to take time. And with the perpetrator dead—" Helplessness battered her.

"You've only got what he left behind for leads."

Scowling, she glanced in his direction. "And you keep finishing my sentences."

David snorted. "Perhaps. Now what can I do to help with dinner?"

With an imperious wave of a hand, Genevieve indicated to the vegetables. "There's broccoli, beans, and chard there. You can put that on while I finish the meat."

"Not too juicy, I hope?"

"No. I know you're struggling with the blood hunger, and I won't gross you out. We also need to talk about furniture."

David waited through dinner, knowing that Genny—his pet name for Genevieve—would likely hit the roof when he told her what he'd done.

He ate slowly, still very much unused to the blue meat. Thankfully, she understood he had issues with raw. He sighed and swallowed the morsel, then took a small sip of the superb chardonnay he'd poured. He knew most would team the red meat with a fulsome red, but tonight, he didn't care.

Genevieve nibbled at the vegetables. "I finished the last of my reports and placed them on the boss's desk. When he gets in tomorrow, I'll need to run them past him, then make plans for how we're going to hunt down—"

"Actually, my love, you're going to need to apply for leave." He kept his voice calm and low.

"Why?"

"I've booked us a plane trip. A holiday, of sorts, if you will." He waited, knowing how she'd react.

"But I can't." She shook her head as if to reinforce the words.

David settled back in his chair and gazed at the woman who'd captured his heart. "I was talking with your father. Padraic," he corrected when she opened her mouth.

When Genny frowned, he sighed. Since the encounter months ago in the diner, she'd made little attempt to follow up, and only when David had pushed the point.

"Why would you do that?" She rose and started clearing the table.

David sighed. Genny might be a strong woman, but she was clouded by the mess her mother had made of Genny's life. First, not owning up to the one-night stand when she'd become impregnated with Genny, then refusing to even tell her who the father was. Leaving her to struggle for years as a hybrid and allowing her to be insulted and cut off by the members of her pride, all of which seriously dented her self-esteem.

"Genny, he's worried."

"I'm fine," she muttered, rinsing the plates before sliding them into the dishwasher.

They'd been down this path before. She'd refuse to admit that she needed to understand that side of herself, and he'd worry himself silly. Padraic's words to him a fear producing refrain.

"She needs to understand who and what she is, David. Continuing to ignore this will only bring her grief and pain. You must make her see."

"And I'm trying, but her mother—"

"That fucking bitch!" interrupted Padraic.

"Be that as it may, she's still Genevieve's mother. She did a job on her, Padraic. Her formative years were hard, and she was kept at length from anything that might be considered vital or important. It's taken her years to find a position that nurtures who and what she is." David had to stop, because talking about Vivienne made him wish she was within reach, so he could lash out. Make her accountable. For Genny's sake, he didn't though.

"Genevieve is half-leprechaun. She needs to learn the lore and the law. Right now, the powers of her magic are contained, but eventually..."

"Padraic, I've been looking and everything I've read says there's no such thing as a female leprechaun."

The man burst out laughing. "Think we'd give away all our secrets, do you, lad? You may be her mate, but you don't know everything."

Padraic's words sat him back. "What do you mean?"

"Our women are fiercely guarded, David. If I'd known of her existence before now, do you think I'd have allowed her to

grow up as she did? Without either home or hearth. A loving family to support her?"

David stabbed his pen into the blotter of his desk. "I don't honestly know, Padraic. I've only met you once."

"Aye, that's true. We leprechauns are fae though. A family long ago denied our true inheritance, so we made our own. We know going without and hard lives. Many of us perished in the mists of time, but those of us who remain? We cherish everything we have and everyone."

David looked at the notes he'd made. Circled on the paper was the word family.

"You need to see her? Face-to-face?"

"Aye, David. She'd been under the radar, but now that Danu knows of her existence, she'll be watching for a misstep. Genevieve must learn." Padraic infused the words with a surety that bit at David.

"I'll do what I can, Padraic. But she's a woman who makes her own decisions."

The conversation four weeks ago chased through his memory. "Padraic says Danu knows about you."

"Danu?"

"The Gaelic Goddess. He says she's watching for you to make a misstep. That it would be...difficult to argue you don't know if you refuse to talk to him."

Genny slid the mug she was loading into the dishwasher and turned. "What?"

"We're leaving for Limerick on Monday. Genny, apply for the leave. Whatever it is we don't know, it puts all our plans in jeopardy until you do."

He searched her face, watching as she blinked once then again. David knew the moment she capitulated, in the way her shoulders slumped.

"Fine. But one week. Whatever I don't know at the end, too bad, too sad."

He released the breath he'd inhaled and gathered her close. "Thank you."

"What for?" Her voice was muffled against his chest, and he closed his eyes, feeling the heat of her breath against him. Let it fill him with heat, and it assisted to ward off the ice that had gathered there.

"For agreeing."

Tugging away, she gazed at his face. "You're so sure that whatever is bad, that it worries you." She cupped his face. "I don't want that for you or us. We do this together though."

"Always together," he answered.

Her smile was strained, but he knew she'd given her word and that was all he needed to know.

Chapter Two

Genevieve clasped her hands in her lap. David had arranged for a private jet. She didn't know how, only that it either cost him a bomb or he'd made some arrangement or deal. Either way, the price, in her mind, was exorbitant. Experiencing aspects of the lifestyle he'd grown up with continued to be downright uncomfortable for her. Luxury and entrée into upper society were things she'd never before encountered.

Besides, focusing on that kept her from wrestling with her emotional turmoil surrounding meeting with Padraic. Her biological father.

She had only met him once, but he'd made an impression. From his red hair and gold eyes, to the presence of the man. *Imposing. Powerful. Dangerous.*

Countless covert hours had passed learning about leprechauns, and it left her feeling adrift. Facts floated to the top of her mind—foremost, that there were no female leprechauns. At the centre of her discomfort was that. If she were part leprechaun, then was she the only one?

"Hey," David murmured as he settled in beside her. "What's wrong."

Tears pricked and Genevieve shook her head. "Nothing," she whispered, but the snotty words betrayed the fears gnawing at her mind.

"Genny, I know you're worried. You've got a scary time ahead, but I'll be there, beside you, every step of the way."

"But I'm the only one, David." The words slipped out, and he sighed, dragged her into his embrace. "Or so I've been able to learn. The only female."

"That makes you unique."

"I'm sick of being unique and different and the only one." Her eyes slid shut in disgust at the petulance in her voice.

"Mr David? Ms Genevieve? Could you please put on your seatbelts? We're ready for take-off."

At some point during the conversation, the young male steward had walked up without Genny being aware, and now he hovered behind them.

She slid away from David and grabbed the straps, heard the satisfying click, and glanced up.

"Once we're airborne, we'll be offering refreshments," the steward said as if he'd completely missed the emotional scene—one he'd obviously witnessed.

David shook his head. "I'll let you know when we're ready. Thanks, Ignatius."

She waited, listening for the cushioned footfalls of the young man to die away, then turned back to David. "I'm sorry. I'm being childish."

He smiled and once again pulled her close enough so she felt the heat of his body nestled against hers. "Don't be sorry. You've a lot to cope with. I just hope this is the last hurdle, so we can run away and get married." He wiggled his eyebrows, and she laughed, the sound wet, but it released the pressure in her chest.

"I really want to organise the wedding. When we get back and sort out the rest of the furniture—"

"Genny—"

"Have I told you how much I like that? Being called Genny?" She shook her head, feeling like she had to make this declaration, immaterial of the worries involved in planning their wedding. "In my head, it's like I'm two separate people now. Genevieve is growing smaller while Genny, the woman you make me, is ready to change and grow. Ready to marry." The bubble of concern inside her deflated a little more. "I... God, this is going to sound silly, but I think of myself now, sometimes as Genny. It's the person I want to be, David."

"Furniture be damned," he whispered, pulling her close as the forces of take-off held them against their seats. "We do the white gown, flowers, and guests. But we do it our way."

"But I thought in the back garden—"

"Is that what you want, Genny?"

She bit her lip. "I'd like the whole nine yards, but you've—"

"That didn't mean anything to me. This does. We matter. We don't start our life together with a hole-in-the-wall ceremony because of Alexa. She's my past. You're my future and the woman I will spend my eternity with. My choice."

Genny couldn't say why she'd uttered those words. She knew Alexa—bitch that she was—had the big society wedding. Not that it was exactly what Genny wanted, but she'd been willing to settle for small, discreet, and quiet for her wedding to spare David the memories.

Alexa had made David pay. Even now, the memory of his ex-wife and the lies she'd told dogged David. People commented. He'd changed his entire life and yet she hung over them like a big, black cloud. Genny would do anything to offset the bad memories of the short and unhappy marriage.

David clearly had other plans. "So, Hope offered the house, if you want to get married there. Or we can hire a venue. While we're in Ireland, we could look at rings?"

She turned toward him. "Tell me honestly that this wedding doesn't remind you of then." Her guts tied in knots, waiting for his answer.

His smile lit his eyes. "Not at all. With Alexa, it was my mother and her making the choices and decisions. I wasn't really involved. The rings were chosen by my mother. The location, time. And meal too. I simply turned up, played my part, and said 'I do' when prompted. There was nothing of me in the ceremony. This time? It's about us."

Gulping, she considered his words. He'd never lied to her, and yet something deep inside urged caution. "I..." Genny wet her lips. "I really want a nice wedding. With photos, and a meal, and our friends around us."

"Then that's what we'll have." He reached over and unclipped the seatbelt before he rose and held out his hand. "Now, come this way. I bet you've never been on a jet like this and there's a few surprises."

"Like?

"A full kitchen. A small sitting room for the staff. A luxury bathroom. And a bedroom, made for sin."

The bottom fell out of her stomach at the grin he flashed her way. "A bedroom?"

"You have to see it to believe it."

The suite—because it was so much more than just a bedroom—was indeed sinful.

David steered Genevieve down a corridor, with the windows looking over the wings, and to the left-hand side was a door, near the end. He opened it and ushered her into a pale blue room. The bed, a massive affair, sat in the centre, with a pale blue glowing light illuminating it.

"What do you think?" he asked.

"It's... Wow!"

David laughed. "Come in here then," he said, and opened a sliding door to reveal a bathing room as large as the one in the property they'd just bought. A deep spa bath sat in the centre of the room, a shower to the right, and vanity unit to the left. There was another door which she supposed led to a toilet.

"On a plane?"

Once more, David chuckled. "Sometimes when the master or mistress need to travel, and are in an unfamiliar location, they use the planes as their personal base."

Genevieve made a slow circle. "That I understand, but this is luxury."

He nodded. "My parents used the plane sometimes too when travelling the events. Status is important among the older families *Yeux Secondes*."

That she understood, having now visited Hope—David's sister—and Xavier's home. Hell, she'd met the new *Yeux Secondes*, and found them to be nice. Normal almost. Though the whole house structure was old and, as David explained, meant to be imposing. "But not all nests are like that. Javed's isn't."

"No. But it's a new nest, so it's yet to build up the structure and years of status, though I doubt either Javed or Celina are that way inclined."

Genevieve opened her mouth, but David dragged her close and sealed the query with a demand before she could speak further. The veil of hunger slid away and he replaced the wonder at the luxury surrounding them with a hunger that roared through her veins.

The kiss was slow and drugging, stealing thoughts, as her body responded to his careful stripping of her. When he lifted his head, she felt hot and hungry. "Ever made love in a spa?" he asked.

Shaking her head, she watched mutely as he stalked over and

turned the handles so water cascaded from the gold taps into the bottom. David slid aside a cabinet door, withdrew salts, and sprinkled them, so the air was filled with the lush scent of wildflowers. Then he turned and started to strip, every move deliberate and provocative. His eyes called her to join him, and she followed his lead, allowing her clothes to drop unheeded to the floor.

Finally naked, her gaze roamed over the miles of flesh, settling on the sight of his jutting cock.

"Genny..." He reached out a hand and she took it, and he stepped into the bath, urging her silently to join him. The water was perfectly warm. Neither too hot nor cold, so as she sank down, it was a whisper against exposed flesh.

His hand touched a button, hidden from sight, and the windows, blocked with almost seamless blinds, opened with a mechanical whirr. The sight of clouds and blue sky caught her attention, and surprise filled her when he reached for and cupped her breasts, gently towing her against him.

"We're a mile high, Genny. Naked and wanting. Will you let me love you?"

There could be no answer, at least not given in words, because his words were a promise, and her brain turned to mush as her body, with nerves quivering, took over. Genny turned, blindly seeking his mouth with hers.

His fingers, deft and knowing, plucked at her nipples, tweaking softly, but increasing the hunger that built like a furnace deep in her belly. His mouth moved, finding the curve of her cheek, every touch a benediction. At the shell of her ear he whispered, "I want you, Genny. I want your body and mind. I want to be with you so much that when we're apart I ache."

She squirmed until she found the best position, sliding her legs over his thighs so their bodies were nearly intertwined. Her hands seeking purchase on his shoulders.

"I love you, David."

Her eyelids dropped to half-mast but not before she caught sight of the glitter of carnal hunger in his gaze. "Just as I love you, Genny."

His hands gripped her waist, lifted her as the points of her breasts, now pebbled with sensual need, grazed against his chest. Lightning arced, and she inhaled sharply as he held her high, then inexorably lowered her down so his erection slid deep within her body.

They moved together, undulating as water lapped across sensitive skin. She arched and bowed, searching for the release only he could bring, knowing that David was there with her. The harsh sound of urgent breaths filled the air along with moans as every slide inched them closer to the edge of reality.

For a brief, blinding flash of a second, she teetered on the edge. "Let go, my love," he urged, and she fell, splintering senses as the orgasm crashed. She felt him, heard the grunt as he emptied himself deep within her.

Then they stilled, holding on to each other as the ragged cadence of breathing filled the air.

"So that," she panted, "is the mile high club entry?"

His bark of laughter filled her with pleasure. "More than that. Call it a distinguished membership reward."

Genny closed her eyes, let the frantic beating of her heart subside, yet it was hard, as her body had taken on the boneless quality of satiation. "Well, that was..." She hunted for the right word.

"Amazing? Stupendous? Brilliant?" He spoke with a lazy drawl, and she couldn't help the giggle.

"All that and more. As you know, Mr Studly."

"Mr Studly, hmm? I like that. Think I'll get that engraved on your wedding band."

"Wedding band?" Once again it was like the oxygen was being stolen from her chest. Only in a good way. Opening her eyes, she stared at him. Smiled. "I can't wait."

While they slept in the large bed on the plane, in Ireland a man paced. Wondered. Pondered and understood the danger ahead.

The trials were necessary.

If only they didn't worry him so much.

He lifted the dark brew to his lips and drank. Nothing more to be done now, he thought. Tomorrow would be soon enough to worry.

Chapter Three

The landing was soft, and Genny inhaled deeply, clutching the overnight bag she shared with David in her hand. This part? This was hard. Meeting Padraic, the man who claimed to be her biological father, in the flesh after months of avoiding him had her guts squirming.

It wasn't that she didn't believe him. It wasn't even that meeting the man for the second time who'd avoided her for her whole life wasn't huge. It was that she'd finally learned what she was supposed to be. Right now, she had no context to being a leprechaun, because as much as she'd researched, the little she'd unearthed was insubstantial.

Questions chased around in her head. No female leprechauns was merely the tip of the iceberg, though it was a rather large hole in what she'd been told. The medallion at her neck, the coin he'd left with her mother, heated as soon as they reached the ground. Not burning but warm, as if it were rejoicing in the return to Ireland.

The airport itself was the same as any anonymous building anywhere in the world. Large ceilings, noise, and movement. They'd entered the private wing, but had to still move through a customs area, though it was shielded from the main room.

The woman waited at a desk, and Genevieve wondered what she thought when she and David appeared. They were both dressed well, black pants, white shirts. Hers accessorised with a scarf around her neck. She wasn't tall, and her features were regular. Her hair, tied into a neat and tidy braid, was dark brown, though her eyes were a golden-green colour, while David was gorgeous. A chiselled jawline, edged with stubble the same midnight-shine as his hair and emerald-green eyes.

"Anything to declare, Mr Jardin and Miss...Miss Fernly?" the quarantine officer queried, and not for the first time, she was glad David was there to usher her through.

"No."

"You're travelling together?" The officer looked from one pass-port to the other.

"Fiancés," David explained quietly.

"Congratulations." The words were banal, as if they slipped off the woman's tongue regularly. "You packed your own bags?"

"Yes," David answered.

"Welcome to Ireland," she said, then waved them through.

David slid his hand around Genevieve's waist, and they exited into a lush foyer, where Padraic waited, moving from one foot to the other.

"Genevieve and David. Welcome home." He shook David's hand and kissed her on the cheek. "The car is outside. I wasn't sure where you wanted to stay, but I hope the gatehouse will suffice."

She cocked an eyebrow at that. A gatehouse? What the hell was that? But asking the question felt rude, so she merely kept her mouth shut.

"That will be fine. Thanks, Padraic," David answered for them both.

"I'll drop you off and you can get comfortable, and later today I'll pop over. We'll sit down and talk, if that suits?" Then he ushered them through the door.

Aware Padraic was waiting for her answer, Genny nodded. "Sure. Fine. Don't want to upset your plans."

He opened the door to the limousine at the kerbside. "Not at all. Now climb on in. Gareth is collecting your luggage, then we'll be off."

Genny glanced around. "Gareth? But your driver is—"

"Gareth is security. He'll make sure you're both safe while you're my guests. Marty here is my driver, but he'll be at your disposal as and when you need to leave the property," Padraic explained.

She opened her mouth then closed it again, in case this was one of those 'later on' discussion he'd promised.

She sat back and took in the scenery as they drove through the outer suburbs. The houses were different to those back home. They appeared smaller, stocky with heavy windows and little to no gardens. Not that houses in town had much more than a handkerchief for green space, but back where the pride came from, the greenery was extensive.

The drive wasn't long, and she looked out the window at the differing scenery. Here and there the road was bounded by houses of white stone. Quite old, she thought to herself. Green shrubbery marked the edges of the highway, and in places, the greenery filled the centre between the lanes. In other areas, she noted rows of houses. Racking her mind, she remembered the term 'row houses' and thought they seemed appropriate.

Limerick itself was a smaller city, with most amenities and housing shoe-horned together until they reached the other side. Now, the built environment changed again, and the area once more took on a more agricultural façade.

The click-click-click of the indicator broke through her scrutinising of the environment, and she realised they were turning into a property. High stone walls hid the other side from view and large metal gates slid open, but not before she saw a large intercom and security system.

"I'll arrange security passes for you both," Padraic said, filling the silence. "That way you can both come and go freely."

Again, the feeling that she was missing something welled in Genevieve. "Why do you need security passes?"

Padraic looked at her. "I'll explain all that and more, my dear, later today."

The car slid to a smooth stop outside a building constructed from the same stone as the wall. It wasn't large, but the cheery rise of smoke from the chimneys, shining windows, and carefully tended beds spoke to a house well-loved and used.

They climbed out of the car, Padraic shadowing them. "I had Maeve come in and lay in supplies. She'll be around tomorrow morning to do a quick general clean, but if you need anything—"

"We'll let you know. Thanks, Padraic," answered David while Genevieve simply stared at the bright green door with a golden knocker.

She reached out then dragged back her hands. "It's not gold," Genevieve whispered.

"No. It isn't, lass," Padraic answered.

Feeling stupid and at sea, Genevieve simply stuck her hands in her pockets and waited until Padraic withdrew. Gareth carried in their bags, then with a quick wave, the limousine drove away.

"Genny?"

She turned into David's embrace. "I feel stupid. I mean, the money. The no expenses spared and the house. It's just..." Casting about, she bit her lip.

"It's overwhelming?"

"Yes. I don't... I'm not used to not having to think about where I stay, or how I can afford it. You soften it for me, but a limousine to pick us up, this place? It just reeks of money I can't even..." Inhaling, Genevieve warred with herself. "Look, I'm just overthinking and stressing about the money thing. It's silly, and I—"

"No. You're right. I do try to make you feel comfortable, but I'm not sure Padraic understands how you grew up or about doing it on your own. Do you want me to talk to him—"

Her hands flew to her now burning face. "Oh, no! It's okay. It's something I think I'll need to work on myself."

David held her close, and she let the solidity of the man centre her.

"Maybe we should go in," he suggested several long moments later.

Genevieve nodded. "Yes. Let's."

David wasn't sure what the interior would be like. It might have reflected the gold Padraic wore in his ring, or his watch, or even his belt buckle. But instead, the house was decorated in a quietly tasteful manner.

Cream and pale pink and green floral paper decorated the walls. The dark wood of the walls and furniture shone with the lustre of careful attention to regular polishing and, most importantly, with comfort in mind. The cushions of the chairs were deep, the fire in the grate kept any chill at bay, and the forest green curtains completed the look.

The hall they'd entered was laid with encaustic tiles of black and white, but it didn't detract from the overall style of the house. In the rooms leading off the corridor, the floors were covered with deep plush carpets, and dragging through the many facts his mother had instilled in him, David recognised them as Aubusson.

"This place is like a museum," murmured Genevieve.

It reminded him of the house he grew up in. "But it's ours while we're here, so we should find the bedroom and drop our bags." Gareth had only carried them as far as the front door.

David grabbed the two bags, and as always, he considered the difference in the bags. His was a premium leather carry-all. Hers a low-cost, synthetic roller bag. It always jarred him, the realisation they came from two very different and separate worlds, yet they made it work for them.

The stairs led up to a small balcony and three bedrooms, each ensuite. He chose the most comfortable, with a view of the trees, and popped the bags on the bed. *We can unpack later.*

He headed downstairs and found Genny in the kitchen, studying the kettle. "If I hadn't seen one of these before, I wouldn't know what it was for," he said as he unclicked it from the base and set to filling it up. Within moments they'd settled into the lounge with a coffee.

"You didn't talk to Padraic much," David noted.

Genny sighed. "I want to, it's just... I mean, what do I say? 'Hey, Dad! Why weren't you around when my mum had to run away from her husband?' I know he didn't know. She didn't give either of us a chance, and I'm still pissed at her about that, but I'm an adult now and it feels all too late. What kind of father-daughter relationship can we have?"

David heard the pain in her voice. Understood better than most both her fears and regrets. "I don't know, Genny. But to find out, you're going to have to let him in." And he sincerely hoped she would. If she could build a relationship with her father, it might soothe some of the hurt she carried in her life. He watched Genny sip her coffee and consider his words.

"I know, but the thing is, what if when he knows me, I don't come up to his standards?" She blinked rapidly. "I've done rejection before, and it hurt. A lot."

Luca Thorne and her mother and entire clan abandoned her. "Just because Luca and your mother are failures as parents—"

"What would you know about failure?" She screamed the words, then slid the cup onto the table. "I'm sorry, David. I didn't mean that."

He was sure she was genuinely remorseful, and instead of allowing himself to be annoyed, he smiled and held up his hands. "Son, husband, *Yeux Secondes* twice over. I know a thing or two about failure." If it hadn't been for her sudden pallor or the way she dropped her head and now silently wept, he might—at a very long stretch—have taken offence at her words, but he knew she didn't really mean them. She was lashing out because she had been so deeply wounded and didn't know how to deal with or process her fury and hurt.

He pulled her into his arms, curling his arms around her. She was a strong woman, but out of her emotional depth, in an unfamiliar country, and trying to build a relationship with a father she'd only met once, months ago. Not to mention needing to know her heritage and laws of her kind she'd never even heard of. Anyone might be forgiven for breaking down under the circumstances.

He'd only just got her to look at him when the echo of someone rapping on the front door interrupted.

Swiping at her face, Genevieve wanted to curl into herself, but the imperious rapping at the door told her there was no break to be had right now. No time to apologise for the slight she'd thrown at David. *Unfair.* That knowledge ate at her, guilt and remorse a heavy load on her shoulders.

"I should get that," she muttered, feeling stupid.

"Just take a breath first," David suggested, tugging a handkerchief from his pocket and wiping at her face.

Heat suffused her cheeks. "David, I—"

He smiled, and the chill that suddenly invaded her chest melted a little at the soft tones and understanding that was clear on his face. *How the hell did I get so lucky?*

On a sigh, she pulled away. "David, I—"

The rapping came again, ever more insistent. "That's likely Padraic. You should get it. I'll have a look and see what there is to cook for dinner."

Genevieve opened her mouth, but he smiled, shook his head.

"Get the door," he repeated, and turned, leaving her alone in the room.

She made her way to the front of the building and opened the door.

Padraic frowned when he saw her. "What's happened? Has he done something?" The man—her father—peered around her shoulder.

"No. He's a good man, Padraic."

"Da," he corrected, and she blushed again, this time with discomfort.

"I'm not ready for that," she croaked and backed from the doorway, allowing Padraic entry. "Come on in." They moved into the lounge, and she settled in one of the armchairs, unconsciously seeking the upper hand in the conversation. "So, you wanted to talk?"

He smiled thinly. "I do believe your man should be here for this part."

Genevieve wasn't quite sure how she felt about that. After all, she'd been alone for most of her adult life. While she both loved and respected David, why was it so important that he be present for this conversation? Did Padraic think her incapable or somehow lesser for being a female?

He must have seen some mulish set to her mouth because he gave her a lopsided grin, one she might have previously found boyishly innocent. But knowing what he was, and the who, it just felt strange.

She pushed back out from the chair and stood. "I'm going to get a coffee and come back—"

"Tea, white. Earl Grey in a china cup would be welcome."

She stared at him, then nodded. It was oddly specific, but she guessed at least now she couldn't say she didn't know what he drank.

David turned as she entered the kitchen. "Everything okay?" he asked.

"He wants you to join us, but I need coffee first. He wants an Earl Grey with milk and no sweetener in a mug. A china mug."

He smiled. "I've just boiled the kettle, so let's get those drinks done, then we can join him."

He bustled around and Genevieve watched, as always, surprised at just how quickly he'd settled in and found his way about. Even more, that he enjoyed the act of cooking, given he'd had a privileged childhood, with servants and cooks, yet he didn't complain about undertaking the most basic of household tasks.

Finally, once the drinks were made, David dragged out an old wooden tray and loaded it with the three drinks, a plate of biscuits he'd found, and some cake slices.

She trailed David back to the lounge and watched as he ensured Padraic was catered to, before settling on the arm of the chair Genevieve chose as her own.

Padraic lifted the cup to his mouth, took a sip. "A good drop, lad."

"Good tea and filtered water," David offered. "Now, you wanted to talk to both of us?"

"Indeed," answered Padraic. "Before we do, let's clear something up. I'm sure you've both probably done some research. You've likely seen that there are no female leprechauns?"

David didn't answer, but her gut burned. "That's true. I've trawled the internet. Everything says they don't exist. So, what's the real story?" she asked.

Padraic smiled, but strain edged his mouth. "Let's start right at the beginning, shall we? Way into the mists of time. Leprechauns came into being long before the vampires arrived on Earth. They were the children of the fae, though usually the ones who were black sheep. Didn't live up to the generally accepted rules of a narrow society. Some wished to be more, others just wanted a freedom that wasn't available to them in a restricted society, where those we take as wives or partners are controlled by the powerful."

She blinked, not expecting such a frank description, given everything she'd seen had merely hinted at those truths. "So, you were a black sheep?"

He shook his head. "No, but your grandparents were."

"Grandparents?" Genevieve felt blindsided. "I've got more family?"

Padraic cleared his throat. "They passed in the wars of the fae, millennia ago. I have no close relatives there. Some exist, I believe in the courts, but I have no interest of association with them."

"Do I have other brothers and sisters? A step-mother?"

Padraic laughed, but it was tense. "No. Many years ago I met a woman, but she was human and forbidden to me. She'd be nothing more than a pile of dirt now, if that." He glanced over her shoulder and smiled. For an instant, she felt the stirring of pity, but brushed it aside, because she couldn't cope with those emotions at this time.

David cleared his throat. "So, you've never taken a wife?"

"No. Unlike you two, my chances and opportunities have been limited. Instead, I focussed on building my home, my businesses, and caring for those who attend me."

"Genevieve is your only offspring?"

"Indeed, and what a cracker she is, David."

Genevieve wasn't sure how she felt about his comment that she was a cracker. She knew it meant great or good, but he didn't know her. Her ire rose. "Hang on, you don't know me. How the hell can you go around passing some kind of decision on whether I'm a cracker or not? I might be a crooked cop or—"

Padraic leaned over. "I know. You're part of me." Then he grinned. "Besides, I had an old friend of Simon Bellingham's send me a report. He told me of your work with the police, and with the weres."

She shot upright. "You had a private investigator follow me?"

"No, dear. You've met him. He did work with Simon Bellingham when Niamh, his mate, was missing. I know her herd. The fairies of the glade aren't strong, and I am the nearest power base they could affiliate with. I don't know them well, because fairies are so secretive, but they live under my protection."

That stopped her in her place. She was a member of Simon

Bellingham's clan, as was David. Did that mean she owed Padraic some kind of higher rate of fealty?

"Now then, let's get back to what we were discussing." Padraic laid his drink on the table and steepled his hands. "You're my daughter. One I knew nothing about until the call of the coin. You know we have an... affinity. Many of our kind find this difficult. Some have been made to pay for crimes because they can't control it, because it's deeper than lust. It's a siren's lure. It's what I fear for you without knowledge or control."

"But it's never manifested until recently. So, surely you must know—"

Padraic smiled. "I wish it were that simple. You've been lucky, clearly not coming into contact with high quality and large masses of gold. The more you do, the stronger the needs grow. And with David's lifestyle..." He shrugged. "The close association you have with the nests will exacerbate that."

"But there are no females. So how can I be affected?"

"Ah yes, women. *Leprechauns*. The stories we've allowed to be peddled about us are crafted. Many we made up and shared to ensure safety and privacy of our kind. We weren't plentiful in the beginning, nor are we now. In the past millennia, our women were at risk. They—and we—were never warriors, or at least not until the wars. Our women were at risk, so we hid them and their skills for their own protection. They became, and still are, among some of our most skilled warriors and artisans. What we have learned though, is once a story which is shared publicly takes hold, changing it may be hard. We have learned—and by *we*, I mean those of us in the Council, still agree—that it was and continues to be our greatest protection. We need to hide our women, so we continue to perpetrate the myth that there are no female leprechauns."

She stared at Padraic. *Lies*. They'd told lies for centuries. What other lies might he tell, and how might that affect her and David? She bit her lip. "You said women were warriors, yet you treat them as if they are weak."

He huffed. "I wish I could say I regret my choices, but I don't. We have so few women and we, and they, have agreed they should put aside their tools of war."

Her lips thinned in a visceral reaction to his answer. The women had become less because it had been decreed. If someone had made her do that... The growl in her throat echoed in the room.

David laid a gentle hand on hers, his fingers sliding over the escaping claws. "Padraic, I think that's about the limit of what we both can digest today. Perhaps, we might have a quiet evening to discuss and ponder what you've shared."

Padraic rose. "Sometimes, it's a case of needs must. We had to protect what we were. We were small in number, and at that time, stature. But this is merely the first step, or the tip of the iceberg if you will." He laughed, but the sound was bitter. "I'll see myself out. But be ready, in the morning, your education must begin. Time is limited as the Council demand I present you before the end of the week for testing."

She stared at him. "Testing?"

"Danu demands it, Genevieve. I argued, but..." Padraic shrugged. "I can do no more."

Dinner, served in the small separate dining room, had been a quiet affair. David watched Genny, well aware she was struggling with some of the truths Padraic had presented. They'd spent some of the evening in the lounge with the television running, and he privately thought it gave her time to think without needing to engage in any kind of chatter. To be honest, he wondered if some of the intransigence was her fear, but another was because she was so committed to truth and morality because of her chosen profession.

Now they made their way upstairs, to the bedroom. He opened the door, and they stepped inside the luxurious room they'd both decided appealed to them.

"Genny, I can understand them with the women," he murmured, knowing she'd need to discuss her learnings.

"But if they now protect weaker groups, like the fairies, they can come out. Like the weres and vampires." She brushed her hair with furious swipes. "Lying is never right." The air crackled with her confusion and hurt.

He settled on the bed beside her, placing a gentle hand on her shoulder. "Some would say witness protection is like that."

Genevieve deflated. "But everything I thought I knew, every little detail I've learned since meeting him, is based on a lie. *Who am I, David? What am I?*"

Tears dribbled down her cheeks, and she dove into his arms, and he held tight, aware that it was the only support he could offer right now. He couldn't make this right for her, and his chest ached at the knowledge. She was a strong woman, but even the warriors could only survive so many blows. Not for the first time, David wished he could grab both her parents and make them see just how much they'd damaged her sense of self-worth.

Her crying jag came to an end. "I've become a bloody weakling in the last few months. I never cry."

He laughed at the disgust in her voice. "Not really. Look at the strides you've been making at finding Julien? What about dealing with the vampires who tried to attack us? You've come to terms, sort of, with your cat."

Swiping at her tears, she sighed. "I feel so off-balance, David. Like I can't seem to find an easy way to get through this mess in my head. I know, realistically, who and what Padraic is. I know some myths call his kind..." She sighed. "...*our* kind, tricksters. But somehow, I guess I thought Padraic would be above all that." She shrugged. "Silly, huh?"

Shaking his head, David slid his hand through her shorter locks. "Not at all. But myth is just that. Not the truth, but stories people perpetrate or subscribe to in order to make sense of things they don't know or understand. I can see why they felt the need to protect their females, particularly if they were cast out of faerie."

"You knew it existed?" Her watery eyes pierced him. "Or just believed without knowing?"

David scratched his head. "The *Yeux Secondes* of any given house knows many things, Genny. In my case, while my father never really acknowledged the existence of other paras, I was open to their existence. I knew of weres and fairies, because, from time to time, they were needed. Remember, the houses have a complement of witches too, so it wasn't that great a step to acceptance of other forces and kinds."

Snuggled down in his embrace, she shivered in the night air. "I think we should get in bed," she whispered.

His brow arched. "First, I'll set the thermostat."

She nodded and moved out of his arms, tugging back the covers.

He rose and made for the door, her image emblazoned in the mirror before him, and he watched, mesmerised, as she unfastened the old-fashioned dressing gown he'd insisted she pack—much to her disgust. Now completely nude, she dove into the bed. "Holy hell!"

He whirled back at her shout, instincts on high alert. "What?"

"It's cold in here," she groused, and unable to suppress the burst of laughter, he chuckled.

The thermostat handset was quickly set, ensuring the chill of the night air in the old property would be beaten back. A blast of warm air from vents hidden near the walls began heating the room as David stalked over, shed his pyjamas, and slid into the bed beside her. The bed was cool, but the heat of her body was a magnet, and he slid closer.

"I read somewhere that two naked bodies are more affective at raising body temperatures than a heater." He waggled his eyebrows, and she laughed.

"Hmm, let me consider that. You're naked. So am I. I bet it works like rubbing two sticks together, does it?" she said. His attempt to appear innocent in light of her words must have been a pale imitation because she now chuckled. "Your face gives you away, David."

David rolled onto his side, so he faced her, and slid a gentle, questing hand to her hip. "I'm game to see what happens if you are."

She yawned loudly. "I'd love to snuggle tonight, if you don't mind?"

His heart filled to bursting. "I'll hold you forever, if you'll let me."

With her in his arms, he waited for her to doze off and wondered what would come next.

Chapter Four

Genevieve woke early and headed downstairs, theorising a filling breakfast would help them get through the day, whatever it brought.

The bacon was sizzling, and she had eggs ready to serve with French toast, and the coffee was brewing in the pot she'd found in the cupboard, when she looked out the window. At first, she was sure it was only bushes, but something about the way it moved had her stepping back. There was an element of shock and fright when she caught the flash of something.

A noise at the door had her whirling, the tongs in her hands raised like a weapon, and the prickle of awareness at her nape urging her to wariness.

"What's wrong?" David's bleary eyes narrowed to sudden sharpness when he caught sight of her.

"There's something out there." She nodded her head to the window.

He turned. "I'll go look."

"No!" she bellowed, then winced. "I meant no. We don't know what it is, but it's not currently advancing. I'd suggest we watch, and when Padraic comes by in an hour or so, then we mention it to him. Perhaps it's something he cares for or has power over. Not knowing anything about it, means going out there and confronting it, we have no idea how powerful it is or how much of a threat, and we could inadvertently cause something to happen."

David frowned. "You're right, but—"

"I know," she muttered, looking back out the window to see if she could still discern movement, but it was gone. Or at least, she thought it was. "I don't like not knowing either. But we're not at home or on strong ground."

After a final glance through the window, she finalised laying the food on warmed plates, and David carried the coffee to the small parlour she'd set at the front of the house.

They ate in silence, and she was aware he was as concerned and off-balance as she was. "When should we expect Padraic?" she asked.

David shrugged. "He texted me earlier and said he had some office stuff to do first, then he would be down. To dress warmly and be prepared to go for a drive."

They moved upstairs and prepared themselves, and from habit, Genevieve looked around for something suitable she could use as a weapon—for safety, of course.

In the way of couples in unison, they made their way back downstairs, cleared the breakfast dishes in companionable silence, and finally, the sound of knocking echoed through the house.

Padraic waited on the front step and noted their heavy jackets and warm boots with a pleased smile. "Come. Today I have plans to introduce you to people, to explain aspects of our lore and to show you a country no one else can see."

His effusive words didn't dispel the tide of misgiving, and Genevieve couldn't help the look over her shoulder.

"Is something amiss?" Padraic enquired, and she turned, scrutinised the man before her and frowned.

"Perhaps once we're in the car, we should talk," she murmured and climbed inside the vehicle. The interior was plush, comfortable, and built for many more than the four of them. Today the party consisted of Padraic, David, Genevieve, and the driver.

They pulled away, and Padraic raised the heavy plexiglass screen. "This will ensure our privacy. Now, what's happened?"

Genevieve glanced at David, and he shrugged, while indicating she should begin. "This morning, as I prepared breakfast, I was sure something was watching from the bushes at the rear of the house."

Padraic's features shuttered, his eyes drooping to half-mast. "Describe this thing," he demanded.

"That's the problem," she explained. "It was more a feeling than a seeing. I'm sure there were two eyes, but what else I don't know. I can tell you I felt an air of...not quite menace, but a negative emotion, like the danger was yet to unfold."

"There are many things on Earth we can't describe, my child. Some we understand, some we don't, and some that are yet to reveal themselves. It's as if the aged Earth is sharing just enough secrets in small amounts to keep us occupied."

The cryptic words didn't ease her disquiet though. Instead, it seemed to fan the flames of ire. "Damn it, if we're in danger, we have a right to know." Her voice rose, and David laid a gentle hand over hers, helping her to find an equilibrium and assuage her fury.

David cleared his throat. "I understand your explanation, Padraic, but Genevieve is right. We came here in good faith—"

The older man sighed and leaned back against the cushions of the car seat. "You are right, of course. A female in our midst is uncommon. As I explained yesterday, traditionally, we hide our women. Though they train alongside us and are exceptional warriors in their own right, we ask them to use their skills to ensure the safety of our young. We don't bear many children. It's rare for a couple to even replace themselves, so our numbers are slowly dwindling, and the few offspring borne are precious to us."

The words hit like a blow to her stomach. *The few offspring borne are precious to us.* Yet here she was, living proof that sometimes things didn't quite occur the way it was planned or expected.

"But you have an idea, don't you?" David's quiet question cut to the heart of the matter.

"Not with any real assurance. At least not yet. The thing is, we have many enemies. We're called tricksters, yet our powers aren't just finite, they're also limiting. We can't go to war with the fae, not unless they strike the first blow. So, we must wait and watch. It's..." He closed his eyes as if searching for the perfect word. "It's dangerously limiting. Many times we must simply rely on our instincts in order to remain hidden and safe."

"But you have an idea," Genevieve spat out.

"Yes. There are several schools of fae, and I'm wondering if it isn't boggart." He winced a little, and Genevieve got the overall impression these weren't words he offered happily.

"A boggart," she parroted.

"Evil brownies. Many are faithful and good, but temptation can lead them astray, as will anger or hate."

"And what do they look like?" David asked.

Padraic cleared his throat. "Well, as to that, they don't have any one single appearance. Some are tall and others are shorter. I've heard them being no bigger than the size of a calf. They can appear human or animalistic." He shrugged. "It's individual really."

"So, we don't know right now what could be out there, just that it's *something*?" Genevieve winced at her sarcastic tone. "Sorry, I don't mean to be so..." She waved a hand in the air. "But if a potential attacker is out there, we need to know what and how to protect ourselves."

Padraic sniffed. "I'll talk with the guardian of the glade. She may know if one is skulking hereabouts."

It wasn't nearly enough, but for now, it would have to do. Genevieve settled back against the cushions of her seat and shoved her hands into the pockets of her jacket.

"Where are we going first, Padraic?" David questioned.

"I have arranged for us to meet with some of the others like us. Now, you must be careful. Think before you answer, child. While today is an introduction, several of the Council will be in attendance. Be quiet and composed and carefully consider every answer before you speak. For everything you say to them will be weighed and measured."

Genevieve frowned. "Then why am I meeting them today? Couldn't it wait?"

Padraic shook his head. "No, lass." His face tightened and white lines bracketed his mouth. "In their eyes, I hid you. Gave you an unfair advantage ahead of the meetings that are to be." Before Genevieve could speak, he held up a hand. "I know. It's nothing of the sort, but they don't live like humans or vampires or even weres. All they know is suddenly I have a grown daughter they knew nothing about. One who is half our kind and who hasn't learned our ways. They take it as a slight."

"I'll be by her side," said David, and Genevieve smiled, holding his hand.

"So you will, but you'll not be able to answer for her, boyo. She must stand up for herself, lest they call her weak. She must prove she is strong and true. Anything else..." His eyes glittered in sudden darkness as the car moved among a heavy copse of trees. "Drink nothing, accept nothing, and take care when declining all."

The car came to a smooth stop, and they waited for the driver to open the doors. Padraic climbed out and they followed, while Genevieve set her mind carefully curating every fact she'd ever learned about the fae.

Do not lie. Do not thank them. Do not drink whatever they give you or eat their food. At all times, be polite and offer due deference. It really wasn't much.

The gathering stood silent, men and women of indeterminate ages, each holding a glass with a golden substance in them. Padraic's admonishment was forefront in her thoughts as a man carried a tray with glasses to her and offered a drink.

With care, she smiled. "Oh, how lovely, but I've not long finished a drink. As much as I'd love one, I couldn't possibly manage another right now." And in truth she couldn't as her stomach was now knotted with nerves.

"She speaks the truth," a woman called from the rear. The crowd parted to reveal a gorgeous redhead, hair falling in impossible waves and dressed in sapphire blue. Her green eyes sparkled as she stepped forward. "This is the child not before known?"

The woman circled Genevieve, who waited, holding the oxygen in her lungs. Her body locked tight so she wouldn't move and obstruct the careful inspection.

The fae female nodded then turned her attention to David. "And here is the mate she's longed for. A strong, caring partner of excellent breeding. A wise choice, indeed."

Voices tittered in the crowd, and a quick glance in Padraic's direction showed him exhaling heavily, his face sheened with sweat.

"You knew nothing of your heritage?" the woman asked.

Sensing a trick, Genevieve took a moment to consider the words. "I knew my mother, knew she was a were. Of my true father, I knew nothing until recently. Then he wanted me to come straight away. I wouldn't. I have a life, one I like." She smiled in David's direction. "A man who values and loves me as much as I value and love him."

"Indeed?" The woman frowned. "You knew nothing of your affinity for gold?"

Genevieve opened her mouth, ready to say no, but stilled. "I had no awareness of it. I chose a gold-coloured car, wore gold jewellery by choice. But I never considered it an affinity. I didn't feel an unnatural need to own more, and I certainly didn't covet any gold others had."

The woman gave a deep bow. "You have answered truthfully. So now, Padraic, I shall ask you. Did you know a child was borne of your union with the were woman?"

"Nay, I did not, Lady. The first knowledge came when the child was given the coin I gifted her mother after that night. I told her if a child were the outcome, to let me know by wearing the coin. She did not."

The woman's eyes glinted. "And when did you first don the coin, child?"

"My mother sent it to me after I met David. I felt a pull but didn't put it on when I first saw it. It was maybe an hour or two after I received it. After that, there was a pull, one I couldn't deny, and the coin heated when I wore it." Genevieve's hand instinctively covered the necklace, and she watched the other woman's eyes follow her action.

"I am satisfied for now. She will need to be presented to the whole Council, but I will grant you until the end of the week to teach her what she needs to know, Padraic of the Valley. Now, there is another subject we must discuss. There is a darkness that has manifested and has taken up residence locally. What do you know?"

David's arm encircled Genevieve's waist, and it took everything for her to not sag into his embrace. She drowned out the conversation around her as David leaned down. "You did well, my love. There were those watching who nodded when you answered." He pulled her slightly away. "But to be honest, the sooner we leave this glade, the better."

Genevieve nodded. "I agree. Perhaps we should make our way back to the car."

Before they could turn, a hulking man stomped up in front of her. "You are the child of Padraic. A leprechaun. He is not worthy of one such as you."

David tensed, and she slid aside, though she took his hand, and smiled to the man. "I am not your equal. I know nothing of your ways, but this is the man I took to mate." The words came instinctively.

He bared his teeth as Padraic stepped up. "Settle down, Gideon. She is already mated as she told you, and you have the choice of all the others."

The man huffed and wandered off, but Padraic watched his retreat. "He's one to be careful of, David. No one has accepted his suit thus far, no matter that he has a lineage many would fight for. Watch yourself there."

Disquiet bloomed inside Genevieve. "Can we leave yet?"

Padraic cocked his head to one side. "Had enough already?"

"Not so much, but David's safety is my number one priority."

Again, David tensed, but kept quiet as they trudged to the car, and it was only when they were speeding away he withdrew his hand from hers. "I am capable of defending myself."

She sighed. "I know. But something about the people and the place told me that was the correct way to act."

Padraic laughed. "A chip off the old block."

When she stared at him, he shrugged. "What's that supposed to mean?" she asked.

Padraic's eyes grew shadowed. "Your birthright is that of a warrior. Your grandfather and his father before him fought in the faerie wars as a general. Never beaten in battle. You carry those abilities well."

"The faerie wars?"

"A tale for later, my dear. Much, much later."

David wasn't a weakling, and while he accepted the fact that Genevieve only wanted to help him, hearing her say she was taking an action for his safety rankled. It made him question just how much she thought he was capable of doing. He also understood this was something that needed to be discussed once they were alone. He'd practiced so many forms of fighting, so he'd be a capable *Yeux Secondes*... But of course, that was something she didn't know. Not really. Oh, he'd told her and shown her, but she never knew the depths of his skills.

They drove in silence now, as if Padraic understood David was stewing over Genny's words.

They pulled up outside a woodland, and David made to slide out of the car.

"David, it might be best if this time you wait here," Padraic said.

The level of frustration inside him boiled higher, and he glanced at Genevieve.

She offered a half-smile. "I'm going to have to be guided by Padraic, David. So, if he says you should stay here, then perhaps you should." He watched as Genny started to reach out then pulled her hand back. "Hopefully we won't be too long."

The door closed behind them, the car rocked, and he watched as the two headed into the wood together, and it occurred to him that he'd been left behind. Was this an indicator for their future?

Chapter Five

Genevieve was sure she could feel David's eyes on her back. God knew she wished he was with her because something deep inside her quaked.

"Why can't David come with us?" she asked.

Padraic stilled her with a gentle hand. "It's not so much that he, as a human, would be unwelcome, but he's a were."

The words were like a stone crashing down on her. "So am I."

She turned so she could scan his face and noted the way Padraic's eyes flashed a deep green. "Aye, you are. But you're also a leprechaun. They can read the power of both. They'll also know you're my daughter, here to learn. But David, for all he's your mate, isn't one of us. They owe him no fealty."

The words, though quietly spoken, had a sting. David was an honourable man. One who'd worked with vampires and weres. Protected the young and innocent, and had even worked with her when the fairy, Niamh, was abducted.

"Is this Niamh's glade?" Genevieve asked.

Padraic blanked his expression. "These are discussions for later," he hushed her.

"Bullshit! If this is Niamh's glade, then they will know about the abduction. They should know the part David played in helping to find her. To save her."

Padraic sighed. "It's not that simple, daughter."

She stepped back physically from the word 'daughter.' "No. It is that simple. If they don't know, then how the hell am I supposed to be honest and open with them? What kind of honest relationship could I have with them, if I not only hide half of who and what I am, but also the man who walks by my side?" Her voice rose to nearly yelling.

Padraic rolled his eyes. "It's not that. Not really. They live by the old rules, where the witch prophesises and the guardian of the glade makes rulings, and all must abide by the directions of both. I protect them, but take care never to overrule them or discount their beliefs. It's served us well for thousands of years."

"Then maybe the time has come to consider that the old ways are just that—old. They were written in times of wars and famine. When there weren't options, and the choices of allies were probably few."

His reaction was instantaneous, face turning hard, and his body tensed as if ready for a fight. His fists balled by his side. "You're talking about new ways. Many of us remember and lived through those 'old times' as you call them. The death and hatred and abject poverty you have no concept of. We remember and are unwilling to accept the new ways because we saw what came before when people tried to change things, and it didn't work. You're young. So incredibly innocent of the ways of our world, girl. A baby without experience. Don't go saying these things around anyone else, they will think you not just blasphemous but also dangerous."

Genevieve stopped at the rancour in his voice. "I meant no insult." Not really. She just needed him to understand that David was her *equal* and partner.

"And yet it was perceived. Keep your tongue in your mouth and we'll survive this next meeting." He stormed off into the forest and she followed, allowing the deepening gloom to cool the heat of her embarrassment.

They met the guardian and the witch, but Genevieve waited quietly, speaking only when spoken to, and at the end, followed Padraic from the clearing. Just before she stepped beyond the group, a woman, soft with a child clinging to her breast, stepped in front of her.

"You know our Niamh. Tell me, is she well?"

It only took a moment for Genevieve to realise this was Niamh's mother. "She is. Healing and cared for. She loves the Lord of Lycans, and he'd do anything for her. Her brothers are faithful companions too. Making their way. They have jobs and live together in a house very close to Niamh and Simon."

The woman broke down, sobbing. Genny glanced to Padraic before she moved in to hug the woman.

"Will you... Would you give this to Niamh please?" She slid a tiny box into Genevieve's hand. "And these to her brothers." Two small bags were deposited in her hands. "I can't contact her myself, but this... These are meant for them when they find their other halves."

Genevieve glanced at the tokens in her hand. "I'll take great care of them until I can personally hand them over."

The woman nodded, then holding the child close, once more melted into the greenery.

Padraic stepped toward Genevieve then hovered and glanced at the tiny items in her hands. "We'd best get you to the car and those safely packed away."

Without a word she followed him back to the car.

Chapter Six

David felt singularly off-balance as he prepared for bed that night. After the glade, they'd travelled to a small holding nearby where some other leprechauns gathered. He'd sat and nursed a bottle of beer while Genevieve was introduced around, not that the others were welcoming. If he'd had to sum up the gathering in a single word, he'd use wary.

"And this is my daughter, unknown to me until recently. Genevieve, these are some of our local representatives, if you will."

A couple of those eight gathered leprechauns eyed David with caution and uttered a quiet hello.

He sat down in the offered seat and waited as she was introduced and welcomed to the table. Unused as he was to not being at the centre of negotiations, it irked, he admitted silently.

A woman with bright red hair and golden-green eyes clad in bright orange overalls slid in beside him, clearly a wife or partner, yet not one of the gathering. Like him. "Difficult, isn't it?

They are insular and unwelcoming to those outside. It's taken me years to come to terms with that." She held out a hand. "I'm Rona, wife to Eldred, the one in the corner with the pipe."

David's gaze settled on Eldred, and saw the instant the man became aware Rona had sat beside him. "I'm not sure your husband is pleased you've decided to sit here."

She laughed, and it was raucous. "Well, too bad. He's a good husband, but leps—that's what us partners call them, and there's a few—meet regularly to support each other. It's not an easy existence, and our children tend to be close as a result." She slid a card into David's hands. "These are my details. We also have a group on social media, and once you contact me, I'll grab your details and I'll add you."

His head spun. He hadn't really expected one of the wives to be so welcoming, not after some of the things Padraic had said. Or the way he'd acted.

"Thank you. We're only here this week then heading home."

"So I heard. You're a were and so is she. I understand until recently she wasn't aware of her heritage, so that will be hard." Rona patted his hand, and he glanced over, saw the way Genevieve's gaze narrowed on the clasped hands, and wanted to curse. "Anyway, that's my job as part of the welcoming committee." She sat back in her chair. "Tell me where you've been and what you've seen for this is a fine part of the country."

Genevieve had been downright standoffish all night, and he'd felt a deep welling of frustration at the growing chasm between them. Glancing out the window at the black sky lit by the yellow moon illuminating the darkness, he wondered if they'd both made a major mistake in coming to Ireland. Until now, they'd been on the same page, trying to work out where their relationship would head, but since this morning all he'd felt was a growing gap between them. "It's probably your imagination," he told himself, but making himself believe it was completely different.

"Were you talking to yourself?" Genevieve carried a towel and was drying her hair, wrapped in the woollen dressing gown with fluffy slippers on her feet.

"I was looking at the moon," he prevaricated, unsure how to broach his concerns.

"I don't remember it being quite this bright at home."

He turned and saw that she was moving away from the window. "It's all the lights at home that obscure it."

She nodded, and he wondered what she was thinking. David felt the need to reach out and touch her, yet even as he moved toward her, she was looking away, rubbing the last of the droplets from her hair.

"Tomorrow's going to be busy according to Padraic," she stated. "We're going to do an intensive history course, so I'm busy most of the day. He suggested his driver could take you around, show you the sights."

There it was again, the distance, almost like a dismissal. "Sure. Or I've got some work I can start on."

She frowned at him. "What work?"

"There's been an issue with one of the engines. It's overrevving, so..." He let the words die away, unsure if she was really interested.

"Oh. Well, let Padraic know when he arrives tomorrow, and we can sort it out."

He nodded and moved to the bed. Tonight though, he felt no urgency to strip down and be close. How could he, when she didn't seem to be as invested as he was? This trip could well turn out to be the worst decision of his life, he thought.

She climbed into the bed, and he watched, saw the way she twitched as if planning to roll toward him. It was a far cry from the night before, and it splintered something intrinsic deep in his chest.

How could he breach the gap? Gods knew he desperately wanted to, but before he could act, she rolled over, presenting him with her back, and he recognised his chance tonight had come and gone.

Time passed and he heard her soft, even breathing of sleep and rose. Being so close and yet so far apart was torture. He returned to the office.

Waking was like rising through layers, but when Genevieve opened her eyes, she knew something was wrong. Rolling over, she hoped to talk to David only to find him missing. Her hand touched his pillow. Cold.

For a moment, fright ricocheted, but how could anyone get in? With quick moves she climbed from the bed and headed down the stairs, looking for him in the kitchen or the parlour where they'd taken to eating. They too were empty.

Tears loomed, but she refused to let them fall. He'd be here somewhere, probably bent over his computer working, having had a brainwave in the middle of the night.

Padding down the hall, she noted the door to the small room where he'd set up a temporary office was ajar. She slid it open and peered inside. David was curled up on the lounge, the heat from the fire keeping the room warm and a blanket hauled over him.

He left our bed and came down here. It tore at her guts. For all they'd walked together since meeting, this was the first time he'd willingly not joined her in sleep. She knew he'd been tense about yesterday, but Padraic had— "Nope. I have to take responsibility." She moved over to the chair, laid a gentle hand on his shoulder. "Wake up, David."

His eyes opened, bleary. "Oh. It's morning," he muttered and slid into an upright position. "I had some work, then decided I shouldn't wake you." His voice was thick with the last vestiges of slumber.

"I couldn't find you."

"You've got another big day ahead of you, so I..." He shrugged. "I'm not planning to get in your way. Actually, I've got a contact in the vampire house in Limerick. She's going to show me what she's working on. May even have some suggestions on how to refine the motor."

The 'she' caught Genevieve's attention. "The vampire nest in Limerick, huh? And she is…?"

"Leora Walsh. I just need to arrange transport and will meet her at eleven. That should give you most of the day with Padraic."

Genevieve bit her lip as sadness speared her. "Look, about yesterday…"

David turned to look at her. "It's okay. I understand. It's leprechaun business, and you have a lot to learn in a short while. I'll just stay out of your way."

Angry tears pricked her eyes. "I don't want you to 'stay out of my way' as you put it. It's just—"

For a moment there was a spark in his eyes, but it melted away as his phone beeped. "I have to take this. I've been waiting for the specs since two."

With a sigh, Genevieve retreated to the kitchen, preparing two coffees and a meal for them both. Perhaps once their bellies were full and she had him to herself, she might heal some of the damage she'd done?

He wandered into the kitchen, running his hands through his hair. She watched, mouth dried as the first stirrings of sensual hunger rose, only to die away when their gazes connected and she saw a new wariness replace the brief flash of what she'd hoped was understanding.

"Oh, you made breakfast," he said. "Thanks."

"Let's go into the parlour. It'll be more comfortable," she offered.

He shook his head. "I'm not going to have time. I've got a video conference in an hour with a new potential nest."

It hit her like a boulder. *If I'm not careful, we'll drift apart.* "Sure. Okay. But, David? We have to talk."

The wariness grew, his body still. "Yeah. I know." Then he turned and left her standing there, feeling foolish and alone.

Her first instinct was to stalk after him, yell that it wasn't really her fault, and now here she was making an effort and he'd brushed her off. Nerves jumped along her veins, while blood pulsed and adrenaline spiked.

Exhaling, she stopped herself and sighed. "And that won't help, Genevieve. Think before you act." Yes, it hurt, but logically, he was hurting too. She'd noted his wariness. Perhaps she needed to give him some space. Time.

Instead of wandering into the parlour, she hunched over the bench to eat the scrambled eggs and drink her coffee. From the corner of her eye, she saw movement and squinted.

"What the...?" Genevieve shook her head, blinked and looked again, but nothing was there. "Maybe I'm imagining it all."

With disgust she slid her fork to the plate, where it clattered. She set about washing up before heading upstairs to prepare for Padraic's arrival.

As she stepped into the bedroom, David entered from the bathroom, a towel slung around his hips and the drip of moisture sliding down his muscular chest.

Her mouth dried and she couldn't look away. Lust, a curl of heat, started in her belly. "David..." she croaked.

His gaze met hers. Steady. Unwavering, but the heat was there in an instant, sliding over the flash of wariness.

"Genny, I..." He reached out and she let herself step closer, so the scent of him filled her nostrils. Her senses attuned to the blooming of desire between them.

Her hand itched to take his, and slide away the white towelling cloth, but she needed him to want her back, freely.

"I..." Shyness, unfamiliar, washed over her.

"Damn it, Genny." He grabbed her hand and tugged her against him. "I hate this distance between us."

She sagged, and tears pricked. *He regrets it as much as I do.* Without thinking, Genevieve reached up and circled his neck. "I missed you, David. Less than twenty-four hours and I felt like I was being torn in two." Hot tears spilled and she let them fall.

He moved, sliding his hand under her chin, and their mouths collided. Ferocity in the kiss, as her body prepared itself for the passion that flared deep and hot. When David ended the kiss, she knew it wasn't to move away.

She tugged at the towel, and it dropped to the floor between them, then his clever fingers found the buttons of her pyjama top, releasing it so the material gaped. Shrugging it off, she reached for the bottoms and slid them down. David's hands circled her body, lifted her, and without thought, she wrapped her legs around his waist.

The slide of his body, deep into hers, was electric. Every nerve quivering as she arched over the iron band of his arm.

"David," she cried and felt his hot breath sliding over her skin.

The scent of sex permeated the air as he moved, stalking to the bed, and down they fell. Into the well of passion as body met bed, the surface undulated beneath them. The rhythm was wild and almost hedonistic as hands roamed over flesh, their bodies entwined, and the sounds of loving joined only the rough sound of exertions.

"I love you, Genny," he groaned as together their bodies erupted into an orgasm that flashed hot and bright.

Her fingers dug deep into his shoulders as she held him close. "Don't ever leave me like that again, David." The entreaty was broken, and he sighed and tugged away.

"I thought it was what you wanted," he said. "Time to work on who and what you are."

While the words were careful, she read the pain behind them and cursed herself. She knew he struggled with his own personal demons. The whole ex-wife, parents, and so on, had scarred him deeply. He hid the damage well, but it was there, below the surface.

"I should have explained last night. Some of the things Padraic has told me... They're difficult to explain. Some of it, I can't share. Not that I don't want to, but there are rules. Things I must abide by. And others, I need to get a handle on before I can find the words, David. What I can share, I will."

He rolled away. "I didn't mean to imply you weren't being honest."

"I never said that, David. But I need to work through some of it first. Besides, you've made some plans."

"Only because I didn't want to crowd you." He spoke stiffly, and she closed her eyes, because these were waters she'd need to tread carefully if she didn't want it to be a repeat of the last twenty-four hours.

"Padraic said I'd have to go before the Council. They'd test my knowledge of what I know, what I feel, and how I handle these things. I have to concentrate right now, because if I don't, there are... ramifications." The words came out long and harsh.

She felt his roll. "What ramifications?"

Gulping didn't ease the lump in her throat. She opened her eyes. "If I don't, then I have to face trials. Not everyone survives, from what he was saying." The memory of Padraic's words scared her.

"What the..." He bit out the words, and now he held her. "Why the fuck didn't you tell me this?"

"Because last night didn't feel... We were barely talking, and I didn't want to throw this at you."

David's snarl of fury was loud. "We're more than lovers, Genevieve. We are *mates*. We share everything we can. The good, the bad, and the things that frighten us. I thought you trusted me."

Her body began to quake. "I do. I do trust you. But let's be honest, last night wasn't a high point for either of us. I'm sharing now, because you're ready to hear what I have to say, and I've had time to churn over it all." Running a hand across her brow, she considered how to proceed. "I need a moment, David. Let me shower, then we'll sit down, and I'll tell you what I can."

Rolling from the bed, Genevieve took the time she needed, washed but didn't waste time, because she didn't want him to think she was avoiding the issue at hand. Finally, they were both dressed, and she sat beside him on the edge of the bed.

"So, let me begin by explaining leprechauns *really* are secretive," she said. "They like their secrets, and Padraic insisted that it's a skill I need to work on. He says I'm too open, and I told him I doubted I'd ever come to terms with that. I mean, when it comes to work and so on, it's simple. That's the job, but there are times when..." *I'm making a mess of this.*

David tucked a stray strand of hair behind her ear. "I like you as you are," he whispered.

She smiled, because wasn't that just like him? When she felt most exposed, he was the soothing balm to raw nerves. "Leprechauns love gold, and secrets. They trade the secrets to build their cache. But some of those secrets are dangerous, and others, including the true fae, will kill to keep them secret. So, there exists a schism between them. A very dangerous one. More than one leprechaun has gone missing because of the things he or she knows. It's yet another reason why they guard the women so fiercely."

He nodded, and she bit her lip.

"And?" he prompted.

"There are few youngsters born. Most of them are pure lines, but sometimes, that gets blurred and new bloodlines are introduced. But they're rarer still, because when young, they are weak. Hunted. Those who take partners, lovers or mates, find their significant other are killed. Usually, it's sheer opportunism. You're different. You have layers of protections. Vampires will step before you, as will Simon's clan and those associated with it. Padraic also has strong defensive barriers, but it means you need to be careful."

When David's face screwed up, she knew the comment about his safety once more came to the front of his mind.

"I'm not a weakling," he stated firmly.

She nodded, and her fingers twined with his. "No. But it means you're more of a target. Something looking for an opportunity to prove itself will come looking for you. You have to be careful, David. Padraic said if you're leaving the estate, we'll send a second body-guard. Because you mean everything to me." Her voice broke on the last words. "I won't lose you."

He cupped her cheek. "I'll accept it because it would hurt you. Now, tell me what you can."

She laid her hand on her stomach, trying to settle her nerves. "He's built an empire, but it is to protect those who are weaker. Some of them are barely civilised, warring between themselves and against anyone they imagine might slight them. It's a balancing game. He wants me to meet with them."

"Why?"

"I think as his 'first born', as he introduced me, he's planning for me to take over from him."

She felt David stiffen beside her. "Is that what you want?"

"No. I want us to build the life we've talked about. To raise babies in the house we bought together." The words were barely a whisper, but clearly he heard them as his arm snaked around her waist.

"So, we need a plan then."

She laughed. "He'd need to marry or whatever and have other children for that to work."

"Then maybe we should introduce him to some women."

"Going to start matchmaking, are you?"

David shrugged. "Whatever it takes, my love. Whatever it takes."

Chapter Seven

Padraic drank his tea and glanced out the door. The parlour he'd long ago chosen for the breakfast room was comfortable. Well placed, with a view of the extensive gardens. Yet it was also empty.

His recently discovered daughter was in a house on the estate some distance away, and he grimaced at the thought of her with David. A good man, by all accounts, but he had yet to determine if the man was strong enough to withstand what lay ahead.

The partner of a leprechaun had to be strong, canny, and supportive. Yesterday, Padraic had begun a process he despised. That of ensuring Genevieve was suitably matched. He didn't doubt they loved each other, but love wasn't enough. "It hadn't been enough for you, Eileen me darlin'," he murmured.

*"But Padraic, I love you." The words were screamed at him
even as he watched her Da marching her away.
She fought, arms wheeling and the movement of her gown
betraying the movements of her feet.
It was right though, but even so, it tore him apart to hear the*

screams and cries of anguish. He turned away to return to his home.

Eileen had loved him and he her. But the truth was she was human, and he was not. In a time when the distrust between their species was at its height, he'd put her aside.

Three years later, he returned from his travels, far and wide, looking for ways to fill his heart and mind. He had caught sight of Eileen, across the market square. Her face shining as she walked, arm-in-arm with another, a babe tucked in her shawl. He'd ducked out of sight when she'd glanced around, as if she'd felt his presence.

The wound was deep, and stayed with him for many years. He'd watched her funeral procession forty years later and mourned the loss of the woman he'd once, innocently, insisted he'd keep by his side.

Dalliances he'd had a-plenty, and Vivienne—Genevieve's mother —was not different, but never before had he left part of himself behind, always taking great care. The night was a blurry mass of alcohol and jibes from his friend, Eldred.

But responsibility bit deep. He had a daughter, and he'd see to her safety before he settled his scores and went back, beyond the veil.

He sighed, sipped his coffee, and let the heat of the sun warm him.

David cursed, noting he'd missed his video appointment. "But Genny is worth more than some damned prospective buyer," he muttered even as he settled into the desk to make his apologies. Business was business, but Genny was his soul.

The computer dialled, the sound of beeps filling the air. The other side connected, and a face floated on the screen. "David! I thought you'd forgotten." The man smiled. "I'm glad you could contact us though. I've been discussing the vehicles with the Master of the House."

"I'm glad to be of service, Marcus. I apologise though, as I did, however, have a personal matter that had to be attended to." He wouldn't excuse himself further, and the man on the screen nodded.

"Of course. In this business, families often come further down the line of importance. Particularly those of the *Yeux Secondes*, but you'd know all about that. Always a mistake, in my book, because we rely on them to keep us grounded. Now, about the vehicle you sent me the specs for? I'd like to make arrangements to fly over and give it a test drive."

David smiled, pleasure warming him. "Of course. Do you have a date in mind?"

Twenty minutes later, with a tentative order for fifteen of the cars —dependant on the test drive, of course—David sat back and steepled his fingers. Business was good when you offered bespoke vehicles with increased safety margins.

Now, he turned his mind to more pressing matters. Those of Padraic. Considering what Genny had divulged, he wondered where to begin searching for contenders to Padraic's affections. They'd both agreed the priority was to ensure the man had the opportunity to meet suitable consorts, given neither of them wished to relocate to Ireland. Not that they didn't find it beautiful, but it wasn't home, and they'd both overcome too much to accede without a fight.

The rap on his office door had him looking up. Padraic peered around the corner. "Genevieve says you need a driver for the day?"

He scooped up his phone. "Yes. I have appointments that will take me into town today. I'm visiting the local vampire nest, among other places."

Padraic's gaze was questioning. "You're making connections?"

He kept his gaze bland. "Of a sort, Padraic. Now, Genny said you insist I have another bodyguard?"

The man nodded. "Yes. Things are a little uncertain currently. There's some disquiet, and I promised my daughter you'd be safe."

"Indeed." David pushed out of the seat and advanced. "I'll be ready to leave in a few minutes. I'll just go let Genny know I'm leaving."

Padraic blocked the way. "She's preparing for the trials," he said, his gaze colliding with David's, who had the singular impression that the older man was trying to beguile him.

"Nevertheless, I promised. I'll only be a minute." He brushed past, but the echoes in his brain, the touch of the control Padraic had attempted left him slightly lightheaded, and once beyond view, he stilled. Leaned against the wall and regained his composure, just as Genny rounded the corner.

"Are you sick? David?" She hurried close, and he took her hand.

"No. Just Padraic trying something new. A bit of mind ju-ju."

She scowled. "He's not supposed to. You're not a lesser being, and I won't stand for it."

He smiled, now feeling almost back to normal, and caught her close. "Leave it be for now. Whether he's testing me or us, or playing some deep game, we need more information if we plan to counter it. Besides, I'm heading for town. The *Yeux Secondes* and I are going to look at the engine prototype she's told me about."

"I'm really not sure I should let you go and meet her without a chaperone." But her grin softened the words.

"And she's fifty at the very least, and not a patch on you. Now kiss me, and I'll be on my way."

It was only when he was in the car and speeding away, he let her words sink into his mind. 'Not a lesser being.' What did that mean in the longer scheme, and how the hell would he untangle all the strings he was sure they were both being wound up in?

Genevieve waited until David's car was out of sight and beyond the gates before she turned on Padraic. "Leave him alone, Padraic. He's not a toy. He's the man I *will* spend my life with."

Padraic's eyes glinted at the emphasis on 'will'. "But he's not one of us."

"And I don't care. I know you're all hung up on pure bloodlines, but I'm half-were and half-leprechaun. Once I leave here, unless you back off, I won't be returning."

"But you promised to consider staying." His eyes glinted a deeper green.

"No, I said we would discuss when and how long. Not that we would stay. You may be my biological father, but I'm an adult. I make my own decisions, as does David. Or we make them together."

"Indeed," he answered, and she got the distinct impression he wasn't so sure about that right now.

Fury spurted through her. "Or we could leave tonight."

That comment propelled him into action. He grabbed her arm and dragged her into the house. "You have no idea the danger you place yourself in, making threats like that. They will kill you and him, then go after anyone associated. It could lead to war between the paras. Is that the legacy you wish to leave?"

Every word was a bullet aimed to hurt. And she reared back. "No! But I won't allow you to belittle David. To get in the way of us. What we are is totally separate from this mess I'm involved in. Now sit down and let's get started." But the words had done their job, and she worried her lower lip, trying to reconcile the threats to the whole situation.

Padraic huffed. "Fine. So, we talk about secrets, of which we have many. We collect them. Information is gold, as they say. We started that saying as well. Because we trade in information, we amass our fortune. A fortune we keep and hide. Grow. Some call us tricksters, which we aren't, we're simply careful with what we tell and to whom. Leprechauns listen and watch, and if the time is right and the payment rich, we tell what we know, all the while aware of our family and those we protect."

Genevieve scowled. "And how do we know when we talk? When the money is right?"

Padraic stared at her. "In time, the knowledge comes. But you must gather your circle first. The ones for whom you'd do anything. Keeping their safety hones the mind and the senses."

"Like David?" She stared at Padraic.

He shrugged, but she got the impression on the inside, deep down, he agreed. Until the day before, she'd have said he liked David, so why the change? Her mind turned to that as she rose and wandered to the windows.

"You're unsure about something?"

She laughed, the sound a croak as she turned to look at her biological father. "Really? That's the best you can come up with? What changed, Padraic? For months you've been in contact with David. Talking, planning, and suddenly we're here and something changes. Why?"

He sighed and rested his elbows on his knees. "It's not about David. But you must be sure. Leprechauns aren't like any other paranormal being. When we take our partner, they remain with us forever. There is no undo. No divorce or simply ending it. They hold the key to our secrets, Genevieve."

"You think I'll change my mind?" She kept the words calm and even.

Padraic winced. "You're young."

She nodded. "True. But you figured without knowing the intricacies of the were. When we take a mate, it's for eternity. We combine our animals. We become one. One soul. I couldn't walk away, even if I wanted to, Padraic."

He raised startled eyes to her. "I..."

"We keep secrets too. As do vampires, and fairies. We all have things we know and don't or can't share. That's how our world works, and you should know that, given your... advanced years." She softened the words, not wanting to insult the man.

"Then I beg your pardon, and David's. I was unaware of the level of the connection."

She nodded and turned back to the window, looking out. A flash at the corner of her eye had her breath catching. "What was that?"

Padraic was up and beside her in a flash. "What?"

"I saw something. Just a flash of black but... It was something. It's out there."

"Stay here," he commanded, and Genevieve snorted.

He flung the doors open and stalked out. Genevieve followed him. He stilled, sniffed the air.

"Shite." When Padraic turned she saw twin emotions on his face —fury and fear. But it was the pallor that truly frightened her.

'What?" she demanded, determined not to let the way she shook echo in her words.

"There's something evil here. Something I haven't seen in many years."

"What is it?" She twisted her fingers.

"Inside," he stated and made a motion with his thumb.

They moved together, as he kept pace with her, then shoved her within, locking the door.

"When did you first notice the whatever it is?" he asked.

She screwed up her face. "The first morning here. We were meaning to tell you but..." The words hung in the air.

He sighed and slid a hand over his face. "We need to see it. I must be sure," he grunted and reached into his pocket for his mobile phone. Whoever he called, answered quickly. "I need Eldred, Aban, and Lonan. A situation has arisen."

The call was brief, then he turned to Genevieve. "Where has David gone? We need him back here. He and you are both in grave danger."

She stared. "What? What is going on, Padraic?"

He slumped to the seat. "One of my secrets, it seems, could be my downfall. Something I learned long ago. The stench out there? The sulfur? It's demonic. Dark and dangerous."

Fingers curling into a fist, she advanced on Padraic and stared at him. "What secret?"

He shook his head. "Ring David. Have him brought back immediately."

David settled in, ignoring the insistent buzz of his phone.

Leora smiled from across the table. "Now Siobhan here, she's looking for a placement. We, of course, heard about the situation in America. The houses and the battle of Attar. All the houses came together to discuss any succour we could offer, but under the leadership of Xavier, Javed, and Cressida, and their life partners, he was overcome." She took a long draft of her coffee. "Siobhan's well trained in legal affairs, and though there are some anomalies among the countries—"

"I'm sure I can talk to the masters. Perhaps one of them has an opening for legal personnel. Or, if she's interested in something a little different, there is room in our growing organisation for an advisor?"

"Well, David, I must say, I didn't expect you to vacate your position. After all—" She waved her hand, indicating the plush comfort of the house. "—this is very hard to give up."

David considered her words. "On the surface, but I feel fulfilled in my new role. It allows me to live my life free of the restrictions I grew up with."

"I had heard you had a change, of sorts."

Ah, so Leora has heard the whispers and is fishing for information. "I'm very happy with Genevieve."

"Of course," cooed Leora. "Tell me, is Cressida truly willing to release the houses from their traditional agreement of fealty? I mean..."

On comfortable ground, David considered his answer. "Cressida has determined that times have changed. Nests no longer need to live beyond society. That thinking is outdated, and since we're now 'out'—" David made air brackets with his fingers. "—and entering into agreements with individual countries, she believes there is room for nests to now govern themselves. She's openly said it's time to release the chains that have bound them to a single overlord."

Leora cocked her head. "But that leaves a vacuum."

David shrugged. "She believes you're all capable of making your own decisions, choosing your own leader. I see that as a positive, to be honest. You already have Councils and a single head. This merely removes a single layer of governance and encourages you all to work together. I see nothing negative in that."

"Well, it will certainly keep Siobhan busy until such time as—"

"She finds alternative employment?"

Leora sighed. "Indeed. Well, I guess we should get down to business."

Genevieve scowled down at her phone. *Why aren't you answering, David?*

She turned back to the window, but nothing showed itself. The stink they'd both noted on the terrace had dissipated, and Eldred arrived, puffing and panting.

Padraic ushered him inside with, "We await Lonan and Aban."

The tough man with the grizzled beard started in surprise and opened his mouth, but Padraic shook his head.

"When they arrive. Then we will discuss it," Padraic stated.

As they waited, Padraic stalked back and forth, his eyes constantly darting around, looking for whatever he thought lay out there, and with every second that ticked by, the freezing terror in Genevieve's guts grew by the minute.

Chapter Eight

David hurried to the car, the text from Genny ratcheting up the terror, his body sweating, and he was sure he could hear the rapid beat of his heart. *Couldn't everyone?*

Once the door closed, he glanced down again.

<David, come home now. Please. Something is going down, and I need you.>

Hitting his hands on the seat ahead of him wouldn't assist or speed up the car, but right now, he wished this bucket could fly like some of the ones in the House of Tudor stable. Vehicles he himself had chosen for situations such as this. "And I'll be discussing this with Padraic once whatever this situation is, is dealt with," he muttered.

The car flew along the asphalt, the driver well trained and the trip smooth, but even so, they didn't arrive soon enough to soothe David's ragged nerves.

Genevieve's mobile phone buzzed, and she looked down, clutching the metal, plastic, and glass tightly, knuckles glowing white.

<I've just seen the message. I'm on my way.>

Exhaling, Genevieve turned to Padraic who scanned her face. "What?" he asked.

"David got my text and is on his way back. Padraic, what the hell is going on? I don't understand, and I don't like to be left in the dark."

His lips twisted. "You'll know soon enough." Then Padraic turned away, looking at Eldred who hovered in a corner muttering imprecations to himself.

Her nerves wound tight, and she looked at the clock over and again.

It felt like hours though only around thirty minutes had passed when David came marching through the door, his gaze seeking hers, then just like a missile headed in her direction, sliding his arms around her.

"You're okay?" he asked.

She nodded. "Yes, but Padraic said you needed to be here. Something's going on, but he's waiting for some others. Then he says he'll explain."

The jittery sensation that had settled over her stilled now that David had arrived. Not so much that she needed him to keep her safe, but to know he was here and together they'd face whatever unfolded gave her an inner sense of strength.

The door opened again and two men, who appeared to be in their mid to late twenties, crashed into the room. "What's going on, Padraic?"

"Sit." He pointed to chairs, and they settled down in a circle. Genevieve in an armchair and David perched on the arm. Padraic in the other, and the three men jostling for position on the longer chair.

The three glanced at Genevieve and David. "Who are they?"

"My daughter and her partner."

The two younger men goggled at the answer. "Gobshite," muttered one.

"Watch your mouth, boyo," snapped Padraic while the other simply hit the speaker with a fist to his arm.

"Genevieve, these are Aban," he said and indicated to the one who spoke, "and Lonan. Cousins of mine. Distant cousins." His voice echoed with distaste.

"Oi, you didn't say that when you were—"

"Enough, Aban," muttered Lonan.

It took Genevieve a moment to work out who was who. Lonan had brighter green eyes and his boyish blonde hair was longer, with a curl. Aban's eyes were more forest-coloured and his hair was shorter, cut around his ears. He was also leaner, dressed in creamy-buckskin-coloured pants that moulded over muscular legs.

Eldred grunted. "So, who and what?"

She'd already worked out Eldred was a man of few words from their last encounter.

Padraic sighed and closed his eyes. "That deed we did for Danu?"

Breaths sucked in. Eyes widened in awareness. She felt the prickle of knowledge on the air and waited for someone to explain.

The silence stretched.

"We told no one," whispered Lonan.

Aban squinted and made a duck face.

The other's brows furrowed at the action. "What have you done, Aban?" demanded Lonan.

Eldred tensed, and Genevieve sensed some underlying fury. "You told someone?"

"Who is Danu?" asked David, and the oxygen in her lungs whooshed out between her lips. Then he smiled. "Or have you told me before about her?"

"I think we may have, but she's the goddess of *Tuatha De Danann*. The..." She cast about for the right word.

Padraic came to her defence. "You're familiar with the Greek and Roman Pantheons?"

David nodded. "Yeah. A little."

"Well, these are the Celtic or Irish Pantheon. Not so mythological as they'd have you believe. We undertook an assignment for Danu, the goddess, many years ago. A child disappeared and a changeling left in its place. It was the family of one of her most faithful priests who petitioned. We knew who was involved." Padraic's gaze settled on Aban. "It was supposed to stay a secret. We were handsomely paid to complete our task and keep the knowledge to ourselves."

"I might have said something while drinking an ale," sputtered Aban, who was promptly, once again, slapped by Lonan. "Stop it!" he bellowed to his brother.

"For centuries I've been pulling you out of the fire, you fecking twat! I told you to keep your flappers closed." The last words were more of a groan. "How bad is it, Padraic?"

"Very. There's an imp keeping an eye on the house. David and Genevieve."

"Feck," muttered Eldred. "Whose?"

"I dunno yet. But we're going to need Danu to intercede if we can't solve this problem quickly."

"Imp?" questioned David. "I thought..."

Genevieve's hand slid into David's grip. "They're real. I mean... Padraic was telling me yesterday about some of the things he's done. The rules to doing favours and what can be disclosed. They must remain secret if demanded, otherwise there is retribution," she whispered with fear. She refused to place David in danger because she spoke too openly.

"Think quick, Aban. Who was there that night?" Padraic's voice boomed.

"I don't know. Some locals, the odd demon." He shrugged, face reddening, and Genevieve was sure he was feeling downright aggrieved at being questioned.

"Which demons?"

"Berith was at the end of the—"

"Shite," muttered Padraic.

"Feck," uttered Eldred.

"We're dead," Lonan said as he slumped down in his seat, eyes closed.

"Who's Berith?" queried David.

"A bad sort. An arch-demon with connections, if you will. He was once a prince in the angelic order of Cherubim, but no one is quite sure about his descent. Only that he's now important in hell," Padraic explained. "Any favour done for Danu and the great *Tuatha De Danann* will always be of interest to Berith. Some say he's the librarian of Hell. Others say he is the scribe of the Devil."

"So how do we deal with this? Who do we talk to, or what kind of reparations may be in order?"

Padraic sighed. "We need to find out exactly what he knows, and why he's sent an imp. Then we make plans. Without that information, we can't fight back."

Genevieve grasped the gravity of their fears, but not why Berith would send an imp if he'd been granted information about Danu and the *Tuatha De Denann.* "I'm missing something. You said it was one of Danu's priests' family who petitioned for help, right? We know it's likely Berith behind this, but why would he send an imp? I mean isn't it Danu who'd have the right to feel pissed?"

Eldred stamped to his feet. "You have much to learn, but your question is fair. Danu is strong here. Her believers and worshipers are strong, so the demons are always seeking ways to fight back. The changeling was one of—"

"One of his own. Zazrael carried the changeling into the house, dressed in the appearance of the midwife," Padraic finished. "Zazrael is brother to Marrer, Berith's mate."

"So? Was the changeling Marrer and Berith's?" She scowled as Padraic shook his head.

"No. If a child ensued from Marrer and Berith, it would be raised up. But Marrer is known for dalliances," Padraic explained.

Genevieve's head ached. "Let me see if I can tease this out. Marrer likely birthed a changeling, a child from someone other than

Berith, and gave it to her brother, Zazrael, to deal with. He brought it here and placed it with a family of a priest of Danu."

Eldred snorted. "The changeling was delivered to the fae. Danu presented it to the greater *Tuatha* as an offering."

"What?" Disgust was clear in her tones.

"Not as a sacrifice, child. An offering. The changeling will be cared for until such time as it either grows or withers. Danu doesn't kill babes," muttered Eldred.

"Okay then. But why would Marrer get rid of it?" It didn't make a lot of sense to her.

"Berith is a jealous mate. A changeling of Marrer with another, would cause frictions in the demon world, and there's already enough reasons for them to fight it out. Berith is keen to rid himself of her, but to do that, he'd want to be sure. Even though relations with him and Marrer are poor currently, if he plans to cast her off, he must have proof or there's a price to pay." Padraic and the rest of the assembled stared at Eldred as he presented his version. "What? I keep my ear to the ground. I've been offering assistance to some of the lesser demons who wish to cast off the chains of their demonhood."

"And the imp?" David said.

"A way to keep track of everyone involved. If they think that Padraic had a hand in the removal of the changeling, then Berith would want retribution. He can't reach Paddy, here, so you're the next best thing. A healthy specimen of humanity," Eldred explained.

David grinned, and she squeezed his hand, highlighting her fear. "It's okay, Genevieve," David soothed. "If some imp thinks I'm ripe to pick as a human, let them. More fool them for not realising neither of us is human."

Lonan coughed to cover his words. "Rubbish."

"What was that, Lonan?" Genevieve queried.

"Well, you are, aren't you? Human?" Lonan peered at him.

"No." David's answer was a single word, and she watched as Lonan squinted and peered harder.

"Then what?" Aban queried.

Padraic shushed him with, "None of your business, lad. Just be sure, whatever they are, they can both fight. You can, can't you, David?"

"Oh yes," he answered, and for the first time, the powerful grip on Genevieve's heart released and she drew in a deep breath.

"He's deadly," she added.

Chapter Nine

David waited as the house slowly emptied, knowing Genny was reaching her limit of tolerance. The scent of the coffee he was making filled the air, aromatic and calming. He might have sniffed it if not for the noise coming toward him.

Padraic followed Genevieve into the kitchen. "I'd feel better if you relocated to the house, both of you."

David slid a glance sideways. He couldn't see Genevieve agreeing to that.

"No. We need our privacy, Padraic. As much as spending time with you is...*instructional*, neither of us is yet ready for that level of closeness."

Padraic opened his mouth to counter Genevieve's comment, and David cleared his throat. "I agree with Genny. And besides, if we move into the house, how the hell are we going to draw the imp out? He'll know we've seen him."

If you could hear teeth grinding, David was sure he'd hear Padraic's.

"Fine. But you need guards."

David grunted. "I'm already onto that. The local vampire nest has offered us four vamps for night-time rotation, and while we're not exactly slouches in the fighting department, they've also offered us three guards during the day. They're highly trained and very discreet, I've been assured."

Padraic wasn't overly impressed, but David didn't give him a chance to argue the point. His conversation with Leora had started a cascade of, he hoped, mostly positive outcomes for the Irish nest. Including an agreement from Cressida herself, to assist them in becoming self-regulating should the rest of the nests on every continent agree to become self-governing.

Genevieve cuddled close, and while the material separating their bodies was a pain, she also knew it was necessary. The four vampires prowling the property meant that the privacy they'd both craved was absent. Not to mention the three others, all human, who now took up residence in the furthest bedroom.

"Leora assured me they're the best the nest has to offer. Even better, having smuggled them in, I can't see how the imp would know they're even here."

Genevieve gazed at the ceiling, wondering how to form the thoughts in her mind. "It's not that, exactly."

"Then what?" David turned, holding her close.

"For years I've wanted to know who and what I was. I should be careful wanting things, I guess." Her voice trailed away.

David sighed. "No one could have foreseen this, Genny. Nothing about this situation is simple or clear-cut. But honestly, we live in a world so few understand, and sometimes, even I struggle with the complexities."

If David struggles, I'm doomed. The thought alleviated a little of the negative cloud surrounding her. After all, he'd grown up in a nest, where he'd had daily interaction with a range of paranormals and was encouraged to learn more. "You knew about leprechauns and..."

"Not all of them, no. I mean, witches and fairies, weres and vampires? Sure. I knew what they were and met them, if not regularly, then enough to understand about their existence. But demons were, I thought, purely a thing of nightmares. Leprechauns were wives' tales made up by those with little else to do but imagine magic being more, I don't know, than what the average person saw or knew. I guess, for all I was raised with things that most humans imagined went bump in the middle of the night, it never really occurred to me that there were other things out there. I took it all at face value."

Genevieve bit her lip. "I'm scared, David. I mean, I want to embrace what I am, but there's more to this world than I ever imagined, and I'm..." Inhaling deeply, she felt oxygen fill her lungs, welcomed it as she searched for a way to explain the fear trickling through her body in a way she couldn't understand. "I'm scared. Not about what I can't see, but what I don't know is out there."

"So, we take it a day at a time. Together, Genny. Because I love you."

If only it's that simple. Closing her eyes, Genevieve willed herself to relax. To drift and be alright for now.

Chapter Ten

Morning heralded sunlight and birdsong. David woke, stretched, and noted the empty spot by the bed that Genny usually filled. For a moment a bubble of panic filled his chest. Memories of their brief estrangement settling like a shroud, before he remembered their discussion and being reunited removed the heavy block that had settled in his chest.

He looked up and there she stood, by the window. He was startled; for the merest second he thought she could have been an angel, with sunlight making her appear to glow.

Genny turned and smiled at him, but the joy was dimmed by worry. "You're awake. I didn't want to bother you, but he's out there. In the roses." She glanced back outside.

David slid from the bed and wandered to the window, thankful for the thick covering of the lacey curtains, obscuring them from view. He peered out into the morning and at the gardens. The roses shivered and moved, and petals rained down to the ground.

"So, what do we do?" he murmured against her ear.

"I've already contacted Padraic. He's going to stay away this morning. Said he'd already made contact with Danu's house and is waiting for them to arrange a meet-up. He's also sent one of his guards to work with the nest guards. Says they know each other, so should work together well enough."

"And we...?"

"We need to appear as if we don't know he's there. Eldred said imps aren't clever, so it won't have occurred to him yet that we're aware of his presence. We act like a normal couple. Breakfast in the parlour, then later, we take the car into town. Our guards can follow on. He won't be keen on trying for us while we're out and about."

Bait. It wasn't a reality that sat well. He was a 'do-er' as was Genny, but they'd need to play the game. Reel in the imp, or even better, Berith. *If he was involved.*

"Fine. So, we should shower and dress. Go downstairs."

Genevieve nodded, but not before he caught the disquiet on her face. "I've never been good at sitting and waiting," she groused.

He laughed and she blinked. Cupping her face, he softened his reaction. "No, my love. After you were attacked by the Selkie, you weren't keen on coming home with me and letting me care for you."

She sighed and blushed. "I'd never before...you know." She waved a hand in the air. "I'd always sorted myself out."

Aware of the lonely life she'd endured before there was a 'them', he could fully understand her reaction now. At the time, he hadn't taken it quite so well. Even now, the memory tore at his guts.

Rage rose in a boiling mass from belly to gullet. One eye swollen and radiating tones of purple and red while the rest of her face was pale, and the grunt of pain she gave when he picked her up had his pulse racing.

"Who the fuck hurt you?"

Her eye, the one not swollen almost completely shut, widened.

"It was a work thing."

Pushing through to the bedroom, he lowered her to the coverlet, then reached for the knotted belt of her wrap.

Genevieve batted at his hands ineffectually. "What are you doing?"

He ground his teeth together at the pain threading through her tone. "I need to see how bad the damage is, damn it!" Control was a thin thread, almost ready to crack under the pressure of the fear riding him.

"I'm okay. Really."

"Bullshit! You're pale, one eye almost shut, and that sound you gave when I picked you up says it's not the only injury. You should be in hospital. Why didn't you ring me?" The last words were little more than a hiss. They betrayed the true level of his anxiety, but he clearly didn't care.

Her hands stilled him, warm and curving over his fingers. "I'm okay, David. I've seen the medic."

"And they let you come home. No one to watch over you. That's not good enough." Truly, if he'd been able to get hold of the medic right now, he'd likely squeeze them dry. She should have come to me.

"I wanted to come home. We're not..." She waved one hand in the air. "There's no actual agreement between us, David. I mean, one night of awesome sex—"

He gathered her close, setting his lips to hers. It didn't take much until she was pliant, skin warmed with arousal, and his lips moved to the spot just behind her ear that always seemed to turn her to liquid silver in his arms.

"David," she moaned, and his body reacted instinctively. Melting with the hunger that thrummed in his veins.

He turned her and dragged her toward the bathroom. When he released her, she watched, eyes hazed with passion. Reaching out, he ruthlessly tugged the taps on, aware they would cover most of the sound of their joint passion.

"Will you let me love you, Genny?" His words slid out, low and deep. A verbal echo of the passion inside him, burning bright.

Her hands rose, sliding over the cotton of the nightwear. Holding his gaze, she shed it then stood there, naked and perfect in his sight. High, firm breasts with nipples almost raspberry red.

"God," he muttered and shed his clothes, aware his body was hard and needy.

Together they shuffled to the shower as darts of electric awareness tingled everywhere their bodies touched. Her hand gripped his shoulder as the water cascaded down over them now.

"Let me," he muttered and boosted her, grabbing her tight backside in his hands, and she wound her legs around his hips. The hard darts of pebbled nipples grazed his pecs as she squeezed and impaled herself on his burning cock.

Pleasure flooded him, the sensation of slick, hot wetness surrounding him. She moved and he held her tight, gripping hips as they bucked against the cold tiles, reminding him of how hot and tight his skin was. Like it wanted to burst. The pressure in his chest grew, ratcheting tighter, and he kissed the firm, slick flesh.

The ripples began, and aware his own orgasm was imminent, he gloried in the sound of her broken breathing, the tension that now wound her tight, then that sudden stillness of precipice. He followed her, his body splintering while his heart felt like it exploded inside his chest.

She slid down, disengaging herself, and his body, unable to hold her in the aftermath, let her go.

The water sluiced over their bodies. Cooling them in the glow of post-coital repletion.

"I love you, Genny."

She looked at him, bedraggled but still the most beautiful woman in the world. "And I love you, David." Her hand rested on the shower wall, and he was pretty sure it was about all that kept her upright, just as his back against this one did for him. His knees knocked together, as if they were little more than weak noodles.

"If we keep that up though, we're either going to die of exertion one day or end up with a lot of kids."

He blinked. "Kids?"

She grinned. "Something like that."

"You're..." His voice sounded scratchy with shock and surprise.

She shook her head. "No. But I think my heat season is almost here. I'm..." She inhaled deeply, as if there was more that she knew and wasn't sure how to explain. "The hunger is more. Bigger."

He didn't and couldn't quite grasp what she meant. The comment battering him.

"What do we—"

Genny raised a shaking finger to his lips. "Not today or tomorrow, but soon. I feel a gathering inside me, and I know that doesn't make much sense right now. It's just... It is what it is, I guess."

"When it's time, we'll..." He gulped. Huge. Big. "We need to get married."

Genny laughed. "You already asked me."

"I did," he said, nodding. "But now we should really start making plans. Get those rings, and—"

"Whoa your horses, David. We've got time. I think." She sighed. "The first heat season is said to be preceded by a long preparatory burst of energy, according to what my mother told me. There's a nesting fever first."

"Isn't it usually...?"

"With animals the need to have the nest ready beforehand is key. With a generally shorter gestational period—"

"Not nine months?" He felt like all kinds of idiot.

"Oh, we're about eight months as shifters, but I don't know how the other side will affect that. I mean, as far as anyone can tell, there's never been a shifter-leprechaun hybrid. Then since you're newly changed it also complicates things. But there's a couple of books that will explain about the shifter physiology thing. I'll order you one, and you can do some reading on the way home." She grinned at him, and a sort of drunken reality wavered around him. Genny reached out, turned off the shower, and pulled him from the cubicle. "You look a bit shocked."

"I... I am, I guess." He blinked. "We should go downstairs. Breakfast. Act normal... Or as normal as I can after this." He dragged her close, set his lips against hers. "But there's no one else I'd rather investigate the future with, my love."

Genny giggled and squirmed away, then grabbing up the towelling robe on the back of the door, she donned it and dashed into the bedroom.

More than aware the entity hovered outside, Genevieve set about her daily routine. Breakfast was served, and she made extra for the guards, carrying it into the small room they'd agreed would be their base during the day. The vampires were safely encamped in the basement, the large area allowing them suitable room for their sleeping needs and to hold their sustenance.

Over her cup of tea, she watched David. He'd been surprised by the information she'd shared, but within her body, there were already changes taking place. Her core temperature rising in preparation for conception. Her body shape changing subtly, with her waistline expanding to prepare for the forthcoming foetus. These things normally took place in human women once they'd conceived, but with weres, they came before conception.

A crash echoed, killing the mood.

"Gen—" David's voice stilled, and her heartrate rose as she dropped the dish in her hands and ran to the source of whatever was happening.

In the doorway she stilled, shocked and horrified to see David fighting, hands and feet flying against the creature.

The immediate reaction was to surge in, haul the creature back and subdue it. She made a move, but a hand rested on her shoulder. It was Padraic's guard, who'd arrived just before dawn, who stilled her. "He's holding his own," was murmured into her ear.

She glanced back, one of the guards watching the battle, and she followed his gaze. David was holding his own, every move balanced and wary, but fear flushed through her system, nerves prickling.

With his last lunge, David grappled for control of the creature, took it to the floor, then threw himself on top. "We need..." he panted, "to hold it. Interrogate it." David puffed again. "And see what it knows."

The guards moved in, dragging silver manacles from the belts slung on their hips. Satisfied that the imp was now theirs, David rose, rubbing a hand over his face, and smearing the blood dripping from his nose along his cheek in a bright red line.

Genevieve's stomach lurched as she dragged a handkerchief from her pocket. "What happened?" She dabbed ineffectually until he took the scrap from her hand.

David hissed as he pressed the material against his nose and nodded. "I don't quite know what caused the change, but when it saw me alone, it burst through the window and attacked. If I'd been unaware and still human..." He shrugged. "I might have been in trouble."

Those words froze the blood in her veins. "He attacked you?" She turned and glared at the snarling beast.

"Yeah. It was like something snapped inside it."

Her eyes narrowed as she sized the creature up. "We should contact Padraic, get him here and interrogate—"

"Might be best if you start the interrogation. We'll contact Padraic and get him over here pronto," stated the guard who'd stopped her.

"Why?"

"Because we won't be able to hold him long. Once his master gets wind, he'll poof the bastard out of our hands and likely waste him. Nolan? Get the camera set up. Be quick about it." Then he raised his phone, pressed a button—likely speed-dial, she thought— and rapid-fire gave his report. "Sir? The imp broke into the house. Attacked David. We've subdued him but..." He nodded then glanced at her. "Yep, everyone is fine. See you in a few." He ended the call, looked away, and busied himself stowing the mobile phone into his pocket.

"Well?" she pressed.

"He's on his way. But you should make yourself comfortable until he's here. He's got news too."

The dangled carrot did nothing to quell the butterflies dancing inside her. Nerves quivered and jumped, and her head ached. "David..." She turned and noted he'd retreated. "David?"

"He's gone to arrange a tea for you both. Thought you looked a little faint." One of the nest guards smiled at her and the nerves melted beneath the burst of irritation. "You should sit down."

Her knees suddenly felt like wet noodles, not that she'd admit that to anyone other than David, but she wobbled to the chair and sat down, ensuring she'd be front and centre before the imp. Her mind blanked for a second, before the questions she needed answers to formulated within her brain.

"We'll take him out to the hall, give you a moment," snarled Padraic's guard as he unceremoniously dragged the creature from the room. "Let me know when you're ready."

David re-entered the room and slid one of the coffee tables in front of her with his leg then settled two steaming cups on the table-top. His glance was like an unspoken question. She smiled to alleviate his clear concern before he dropped beside her on the seat.

"Thanks," she muttered and scooped up the cup and gratefully sipped, the heat of the liquid on her tongue and down her throat giving her another moment to settle the nerves.

Padraic burst into the room. "Genevieve?"

She rolled her eyes. "We're okay, as you can see."

"Aye," he barked, but his gaze took in the signs of battle, the still present swelling on David's face, and the cups of tea on the table. "Well then, time's wasting. We should get to interrogating this piece of shite."

Her eyebrow rose in surprise. "Umm, sure." Until now, he'd seemed together. Urbane with an air of self-sufficiency. That was stripped away as the guards returned the creature to the centre of the room, and Padraic stalked over to the creature. "Danu knows you're here. Who's your master?" Magic rippled through the air, compelling and dangerous.

"No master," the guttural tones on the creature answered.

"You have a master or a debt. Which?" Padraic growled.

The creature pushed up from the ground, hissing as the manacles obviously rubbed against his skin. "No master. Debt."

Genny stood, circled the creature, her mind furiously working through what she knew and formulating questions. "Who do you owe the debt to?" she queried, and the imp glanced at her and hissed. "Answer me!" Her voice rose, and he arched back as if she'd struck him.

The creature squirmed. "*Berith.*"

"Shite," Padraic snarled and turned back toward her. "What we thought."

Her mind raced. "What is your debt?"

"Freedom from netherworld. Have child. Human. Must find."

"A succubus?" Padraic demanded.

"Never!" The snarl erupted from between tight lips. "Human and imp. Child. Young."

"What, of Marrer? Is she involved?" Padraic queried, and the imp turned grey before their eyes.

"Marrer evil. Marrer kill. Kill own offspring and *impure.*" A wealth of hatred filled the last word, and Genevieve considered the answer.

"Did Marrer kill her own child? Who was the father, and why does Berith use that to hold you to his service?" Her memory of the conversation with Lonan and Aban from the day before rattled around in her brain.

"Marrer kill child not of Berith. She mate with Berith but dally. Not know who sire of child. Berith sent me here, offered to help find, save child of Vinta." He aimed a misshapen hand to himself. "Is worried Marrer know I know about death. Need sent away. Need to know what Danu knows about swap child."

Genevieve blinked. The information was damning. Berith then knew about the swap of Danu's priests' child. "So, she killed the child by sending it to Danu. Right? Then Berith got wind that Marrer sent her child to Zazrael because the child wasn't Berith's. He overheard the truth in the drinking house and sent you—" She waved to him. "—who owes a debt to Berith, because Berith offered to save his child. Have I got that right?"

The imp nodded.

"So, why—"

David's hand snaked into hers and squeezed. "You were sent here to keep track. You thought we'd be an easy target because we're human. Is that right?"

The creature merely grunted, and Padraic bared his teeth. "Answer him."

"Unsure. Marrer evil. Berith want free. Vinta want free. Berith help Vinta."

"You're Vinta?" David asked, and the imp nodded. "Why Vinta? Why is Berith releasing lesser demons like you?"

Genevieve scanned David's face, looking for some understanding.

"Berith regret—"

A cloud rose beyond the door, acrid and foul. It swirled like a dervish, and Vinta gulped audibly.

A body appeared, muscular and black with red slashes. Clearly male, the entity within it took shape, stretching and filling out. Near seven feet with ebony skin which then disappeared behind loose cotton pants, slide-on shoes, and a crisp linen shirt. If it wasn't so odd, Genevieve would have laughed at the sight before her.

"Vinta, I told you to stay hidden." The voice was drawling and heavily accented.

"Lord Berith." Vinta shook, head bowed as the creature quivered, before dropping to a low obeisance on the ground.

"Get up. I'm not Marrer." The words oozed frustration. "I don't kill because you didn't follow orders."

"You said—"

"Yes, yes." Dismay oozed from the words. "I know. A moment of frustration. Well, I guess what's done is done." The man-demon she guessed was Berith squared his shoulders. "You're Padraic. And this is your daughter and her mate."

Padraic's mouth hung open. "Berith?"

"For my sins, yes. I cannot remain long. If I'm detected...well, suffice to say Danu and I are not friends." He stepped to the open door and stopped just on the edge. "I'd request entry, but I guess that would be denied?"

"There'll be no demons granted entry in my home," Padraic growled.

Berith raised his hands. "As you will."

"Why are you here?" Genevieve rose and stepped toward the door, David grabbing her hand. She looked down to his fingers twined around her own then to his eyes, which were clouded with concern. "It's okay. I'm in control of myself, David," she assured him, aware his concern was that she was being magically coerced. Untangling herself, she took another step forward.

Berith tasted the air, mouth opening and a forked tongue sliding out, before retreating. His eyes glowed. "Leprechaun. Were." He frowned. "*Both?*"

She stilled, unsure now what to do, faced with a magic far stronger than the little Padraic had exhibited.

"Yes. But she carries the protection of Danu." Padraic stepped up beside her.

"And she's not alone." David's hand curled around her shoulder.

Berith cocked his head to one side. "No. Not alone. I'm curious, what is it you think I want?"

"I don't know," answered Padraic.

Good, she thought, because neither did she.

He sighed heavily. "Zazrael and Marrer are growing stronger.

They seek to overcome the Great One, Lucifer. Danu has no love for him, but he keeps the balance on his side as does Danu. As do all of us aligned."

"So why did you allow a changeling?" Genevieve demanded before her brain kicked into gear.

Berith blinked. "Dear child, that has not occurred for many, many years. Padraic?"

She heard her biological father beside her exhale heavily. "It didn't occur recently, Genevieve. One of the things you'll learn as you get older, we talk in hundreds and thousands of years. Sometimes in millenia. The changeling was many hundred years ago."

The knowledge settled heavily. *Hundreds of years ago.* Would she ever be able to truly understand and belong in the odd half-world she now inhabited?

"And so?" David questioned.

"I know you...or of you. You were with the vampires and now here? You smell like a were also."

David didn't say anything, simply kept that look of 'so what' on his face.

Berith grinned. "One day you may be quite formidable, but now? You're an infant. However, I will satisfy your curiosity, David of Tudor."

She felt the twitch David gave, but outwardly there was no sign of his discomfort or surprise.

"Marrer has changed in the last millenia. Her interests have become self-serving. She spends more time with Zazrael, which at the beginning I had no qualms about. But Zazrael is power hungry, and it seems together they've made plans to overthrow the system of balance. Danu's followers are weakening, or at least her grip on the human believers. There is more love for smashed avocado—" And didn't his disgust just drip, she thought. "—than there is for worship and inner learning. Marrer has seen this and takes advantage. She imagines a world where she will rise up with her brother, perhaps even as his second, and wield the power of death." His eyes glinted with flames of scarlet and gold, and she shivered at the visage.

He grunted, watching her. "Imagine a world without balance or without justice. Anarchy reigning. While Lucifer may be the opposite of the human God or the pantheons of gods, he too has a part to play in ensuring the balance of all. There will be no balance with Marrer and Zazrael. They align themselves with those who have no conscience and no wish to be made accountable."

"And the child?" Padraic's question had Berith turning, his face pained.

"No child should suffer. Not even Marrer's. Not by my hand. Yet it was no child of mine. I have..." His face crumbled, and his grief flowed like waves on the air. "I had a child once. Long ago. She died, and now I have no heir. She was not Marrer's, but Balala's. My first bride."

A chink of understanding dawned in Genevieve's mind. "She died? Was..." But she didn't finish the query that rose.

"Yes." There was a wealth of pain contained in the single word.

Perhaps Marrer been involved in the death of Balala or the child? But even more devastating was realising if Marrer got what she wanted, then there wouldn't be any hope of a quiet future.

Padraic shook his head. "We cannot be involved. You know the rules, Berith. You must talk with Danu."

"She will not speak directly to me without a trusted source making contact first, Padraic. I've heard tell you are in the inner circle. One she listens to and will believe."

Padraic winced. "Perhaps. I will make the contact for you, but I cannot promise more. I have a child too." He waved to Genny, and she instinctively bristled.

"I'm not a weakling—"

"No, that you aren't, but you haven't yet embraced your heritage and cannot control your magics, nor do you know them all. You are part were, and if that dilutes your strength..."

Genevieve didn't even attempt to control the growl that rose.

"She is strong," muttered Berith.

Padraic frowned. "Not enough," he said, and Genny wondered if there was another, deeper conversation taking place without her.

The demon Berith shook his head. "Will you talk with Danu?"

Padraic tilted his head to the side. "I will, on one condition. My daughter and her man are not involved, are protected."

Berith winced. "I cannot promise that. I will watch over her though, or send those I trust. If the need arises, she will be protected by mine. I cannot offer more."

Padraic nodded, his face tight. "Then I will talk with Danu. How will I make contact with you?"

Berith reached into his pocket and drew out a business card. "Ring the number, tell them you need me. They'll know how to find me."

Sulfur filled the air, thick and cloying, and with a wave of his hands, both Berith and Vinta disappeared from view.

"A business card?" Genevieve blinked. *The hidden world is stranger than the one I know.*

David laughed. "Makes sense really."

"Prat," muttered Padraic under his breath, then the guards who'd waited just beyond the house stepped back, leaving them alone.

"What now?" Genny pinned Padraic with a glare.

"We make plans. You take the test then go home. I need to know you're safe."

She bristled, and David squeezed her fingers lightly. "I'm not sure Genny is incapable of protecting herself and likely doesn't appreciate—"

"I can speak for myself, David." But she softened her words as she shook her head. "But yes, what David was saying."

Padraic growled. "This. This is why I won't ever let a woman get the better of me," he muttered. "When things die down, I'll come visit. And as you'll need some sort of training, I'll arrange for you to meet with fairies in a glade in—"

"I think it might be easier if my alpha does that. He's married to a...she was a fairy." And her mind brought up the image of Niamh, slender and light with golden hair, but it was quickly replaced by the bloodied and battered visage from when she'd been located after her abduction.

"Ah. Yes, of course. Now I'll go talk to Danu. Make arrangements, but the boys will stay here as guards."

Genevieve opened her mouth to remonstrate, but David touched her arm.

"Sure," she answered.

Chapter Eleven

Two days later

David watched Genny intently when she returned from the trials. Her face pale and drawn with, he thought, exhaustion.

"Genny?"

"I'm just tired, David. I need to lie down." She trailed up the steps, feet dragging as she went.

He followed behind, and once she was settled in the bed, he pulled up the quilt so she would be warm.

"When I wake up, we can make plans to go home," she muttered, eyelids dropping.

He held her hand until she was asleep. Waited a little more, gazing at her face, before rising and carefully shutting the door.

Even as he descended the steps, he was punching in Padraic's number on his mobile phone, then raised it to his ear.

"David. She got home safely then?"

"Yes. What the hell did they do? She's out like a light, upstairs." Silence met his demand. "Padraic?"

"It's taxing, the tests. Usually, they conduct them over a series of days. She didn't have that luxury, my boy."

"So?"

Silence again, and David's ire rose.

"Padraic?" The growl now became a demand for answers.

"You should ask her when she wakes. But I will tell you, she passed."

The knot inside his gut loosened. "I'm planning on organising a flight home. Day after tomorrow, but we have some things—"

"I'd rather you stay on the estate, David. Both of you. I spoke with Danu last night. She's furious and worried, and it seems Berith isn't the only one approaching her. I want you both home as soon as possible, but safe. Things are... They're on a knife edge, boy."

"We are planning on ordering rings." And David would be damned if they'd be unable to achieve that one single task that they'd both finally agreed was important to them.

"Rings, you say? I know a jeweller. I'll send for him to pop around and see you tomorrow. I'm sorry, my boy. I know it's not quite what you planned." His voice was low and mournful, as if he really did empathise with the situation.

They'd hoped for a day to window-shop and just be. This wasn't quite the same, but he could understand Padraic's concern...at least in small measure. "Do you think Marrer will try—"

"She's already been attempting to break the wards at the gates. Twice. Today."

David blinked. "Okay. But at home—"

"I've been in touch with your family members and your Vampire Queen, Cressida. They're ensuring your vehicles and homes are properly warded, and your alpha has offered you both protection. He thinks highly of both of you. I got the impression he owes some kind of a debt."

Ire rose inside David, and he had to wash it off. He wasn't a child, incapable of protecting himself or his mate, but this was bigger and infinitely more dangerous than anything they'd faced before.

It'll be hard, but you can do it, David. Just remember, Padraic is helping.

Through a constricted throat, David answered, "Alright then. We'll meet your jeweller tomorrow."

The whisper of Padraic exhaling down the line settled his nerves only slightly. "Good."

Hanging up, David considered the situation. Danger was all around, things they had little understanding of, and they'd need guidance if they were to be of assistance in the matter. Anything less would anger both Genny and himself.

Genevieve woke, feeling sluggish. Stretching, she yawned and crawled from the bed, blinking rapidly. Checking her watch, she noted it was nearly six in the afternoon. "Fuck!" *This isn't the way I planned to spend the day.*

A quick trip to the bathroom, then splashing water on her face, she looked in the mirror.

"The tests took more out of me than I expected."

The magic that she now knew sat just below the skin of her fingers prickled. Sensations raced through her body, and she sagged against the counter. Mere weeks ago, she hadn't an inkling she could do as much as she now knew, and as if reading her mood, the gold coin hanging around her neck warmed and pulsed.

"Genny? You're awake?"

David slid the bathroom door open as she called out, "I'm here in the bathroom. Got a minute?"

He entered and scanned her face. "Everything okay?"

Tears pricked, the sudden rising emotion strangely battering her. "I... Uh, yes and no."

As if understanding her confusion, he waited, hip leaned up against the surround of the door. "Want to talk about it?"

She did, but where to even begin, and what could she actually say which would explain? They hadn't forbidden her from talking with him, and if they had children—*oh Gods*—she'd have to be able to tell them what was to come...

Genny shook her head, hoping to ward off the confusion clouding her mind. "I passed. It was a squeak, but Padraic put up a spirited defence that I'd barely had time to learn as much as I had." She waved her hand in the air. "I can control gold and precious metals. I can smell it, David. And the magicks... I can make things and people disappear and reappear. I can..." She gulped. "I can kill too. With a touch."

He blinked. "Okay, so don't get angry with the postman," he joked, but there were new lines creasing his eyes and worry washed off him. If she read it correctly, it wasn't for himself, but for her.

"I can control it, but to know I have that..." Genevieve breathed out heavily. "On a bright note, Danu says I will live a very long life. Like a long, long time. Multiple times the lifespan of the average were. And because we're joined by blood, she thinks you'll have the same now. You may even have acquired some ju-ju powers."

"Ju-ju powers, huh?"

She shrugged, worried that he didn't seem a bit fazed by her announcement. "And our kids will too."

He nodded. "Okay then. So, what next? I mean, for you learning to use your ju-ju powers?"

"Padraic thinks I'd be better with the fairies at home. He says as keepers of the lore and because they owe fealty and so on, they would be best for the next part of my training. So, I guess we go home?"

"I've got the flights organised for the day after tomorrow."

She waited, sure he had something else he planned to tell her. Anything.

The silence stretched between them, winding the frustration inside her tighter. "Well?" she said.

"A jeweller is coming by tomorrow. We can design our rings."

Now it was her turn to stare. "Rings? I..." She was still groggy and deep thought was a struggle.

"Wedding. Engagement. Whatever you want." He thrust his hands deep into his pockets, something she realised meant he was uncomfortable but attempting to hide his uncertainty.

"I... We were going to go shopping."

"About that. Padraic thinks it's safer this way. Marrer's tried a couple of times today to get through the wards."

She opened her mouth, but he raised a hand he'd slid from his pocket, stopping her.

"When we go home, there's layers of security around the house. She's dangerous, and we can't fight her off by ourselves. He's not interfering, simply allowing us to live our lives without that danger looming over us."

A slow burn started in her gut, and for a moment, she could swear a shimmering red glaze settled over her vision. "Really?"

"We need to be sensible, Genny. We're not without skills, but after Berith, I understand the danger a little better now. We can't fight her and win by ourselves, and according to Padraic, Danu's been approached by others about her. Marrer."

"Maybe we should stay then. Help in—"

David swooped in, sliding his hands around her and tugging her close. "We have to go home. I know this sits badly, but Padraic needs both hands free to fight. You know that. You're also a protector. This time though, you're going to have to let him do his job."

Her eyes burned. She knew David was right, but for so long she'd been the one to fight. To protect. "I..."

"I know. It's hard to give up, but we're only going to get in the way, I think. We should step back, but it doesn't mean we won't help if needed. We make the offer, and we train and learn. We control what skills we have and learn to use them better."

"Yeah." But it still bit deep.

Chapter Twelve

oming downstairs in the morning was...well, anticlimactic. Instead of getting ready for a day of seeing what there was in the shops, of browsing antique stores and hearing the liquid voices of the regular people shopping in the town, today, they would remain indoors. Locked away.

She'd agreed to David and Padraic's request, because she did understand their fears and concerns. "Doesn't make it easier though," she muttered to herself as she rattled around in the kitchen.

Hands slid around her waist, and the scent of David wrapped itself around her. "I love a woman in the kitchen," he growled against her ear, and she giggled.

"Well, I like a man who knows how to use a utensil." She turned and waggled her eyebrows, and he laughed as she burrowed into his embrace. "What time—"

He cut off the words with a kiss that zinged all the way to her toes and back again as she melted in the heat of passion.

The sound of a throat clearing had them springing apart. Padraic watched, his mouth smiling, but in his eyes she detected a sadness. "Oh...uh."

"I didn't intend to barge in, but I knocked, and no one answered. Uh, I can leave if you wish to..."

Genny blushed, felt the scorch on her cheeks, and she lifted her hands.

"Been a while for you, has it, Padraic?" David drawled.

"What?" Padraic growled.

"Since you had much to do with couples. You know, because just letting yourself in can lead to some sights you don't need to see." David smiled, and even through her embarrassment she couldn't miss the glint of humour in his gaze.

"Aye, well, perhaps it has, but the jeweller will be here in a few minutes. She's fitting you in around some other clients and asked me to let you know."

"I'll, uh, put the kettle on," mumbled Genevieve, and she turned away, hoping she could control the unfamiliar embarrassment he seemed to cause in this kind of situation. *Sure, he might be my biological parent, but still... We were kissing. Maybe about to get a little more hot under the collar. He might have walked in and found us... Oh Gods!*

She opened the kitchen cupboards, the fridge too, and refused to turn around while the two men puttered around behind her.

"We'll just take this through to the dining room, Genny," David said.

Still cringing inwardly, she waved a hand. "Sure. I'll have a carafe of coffee, some cream and sugar to bring through. And tea too."

She'd already lined up the cups and spoons on an old tray, and poured the steaming water into the jugs. With a final heavy sigh, Genny popped them on the tray and hefted everything.

By the time she had laid it down on the table she felt calmer. More balanced, and as the sound of a knock on the door echoed, she was ready for the task ahead.

The older lady wobbled into the room, her wild tangle of grey hair ruthlessly tugged back in a messy ponytail. "Well, Padraic. Never thought I'd see the day I'd be designing a ring for you. Better introduce me to your lady." She grinned, pale blue eyes shining with glee.

"It's my daughter." Padraic extended a hand toward Genny, and David wanted to laugh at the comical look of surprise on the woman's face. "Her fiancée and she wanted their rings to be made in Ireland."

"Daughter," she squeaked, as the one arm not carrying a large case flapped.

"Come, sit down, Nora. We need your expertise. Genevieve and David, I'd like you to meet Nora. She's been designing jewellery for many years. Even has a few pieces that the queen wears, not that it's talked about much. She doesn't like it if you advertise too widely, you know."

Nora simply rolled her eyes. "Yet he tells everyone he offers my services to. Well then, let me get a good look at you both before we begin. Stand up."

Feeling stupid, David did as requested, and noted Genny did so too, though slowly.

"Hmm. Nothing too big or clunky I'm guessing. And in gold." She nodded knowingly in the direction of Genny's coin, then slumped into a seat, dropping her bag with a thud to the floor. "Now, just let me get my sketch pad out." She bent over and David took the opportunity to look at Genny with a non-verbal 'what the hell has he got us into' look.

Genevieve merely pursed her lips, steepled her hands, and waited.

With a loud sigh, Nora slid her sketch book to the table and peppered them with questions about their lives, what they did and what they wanted from their future, and at a point about fifteen minutes in, he noted her hands clutched a pencil and moved, drawing sharp lines on the paper.

The more they talked, the faster she sketched. "Well now, let's take a look, shall we?" Then she angled the book up and out of their view. "Very interesting. Let's see." She bent down again, shuffled through her bag, and lifted a wood box. "Yes, I think this might be it."

By now, David could barely contain himself, the whole scenario feeling impossibly strange.

"Well, I have listened to you both and this is what I see. An engagement ring of gold, a single central emerald surrounded by chips of citrine, tourmaline, sapphire, diamond, and ruby." She slid the book across the table.

David's gut seized.

Genny sighed. "It's..."

"Perfect," he concluded.

And indeed, it was. The ring wasn't ostentatious. It was drawn in proportion to the hand it was sketched onto, and he had the feeling of light and energy. Hope.

"Now, I brought these stones for you to view. From Padraic's description I simply allowed myself to pick what I felt might be right." She drew out a lovely, perfect emerald, which shimmered in the light, then added other stones and laid them around the central one. "See how they shine? Yes, if you're happy, I can have this completed in the next few days. I understand there's a bit of a rush on it."

"I... David? I love it." Genny's eyes shimmered.

"That's the perfect ring," David agreed with a smile. "Thank you, Nora."

"Excellent. Now, as to bands. You both will wear one?" Nora enquired.

"Yes," answered David.

Once more her hands began to move over the paper, but this time there was silence apart from the scratch of lead on parchment. She moved the pad onto an angle, inspected it, made a few more lines. "Simple. Elegant."

The page was turned back to them, and it was. Genny's ring was a woven mass of strands, perfectly shaped to sit beside the engagement ring. Meanwhile, his was bold and wide. No engraving.

"I will also engrave inside. Forgive me, that is always a gift to my client. But trust me, it will suit your personalities."

He wanted to remonstrate then subsided, because she'd already captured them here, sitting around the table.

"It's alright, David. I understand your fears. Some around here call me fey, and others think me merely a reader of people and emotions. Trust me when I say I can read you and Genevieve already, like I can my own hand." She smiled and rose. "Now, Padraic, once again I must begin waiting for you. Don't take too long, boy."

"Even after three hundred years, you still call me boy. I'm older than you," Padraic groused.

Nora chuckled. "I'll arrange their delivery to you as soon as they are complete. Padraic, you'll be paying—"

"Over my dead body," growled David. "I'll have the bill and it'll be settled immediately."

She reached over and patted David on the cheek. "I like you and your lady too." Then she bent, shuffled everything into her bag, and tottered out the door.

"That was...unusual," whispered Genny as she reached out and clasped David's hand. "Oh, we didn't offer drinks."

Padraic, who'd followed Nora outside, returned just as Genny spoke. "She wouldn't have drunk them anyway." He settled back at the table. "So, you leave tomorrow."

Genny smiled, but David noted the shimmer of tears in her eyes. "Yes."

David cleared his throat. "You'll be welcome to join us—"

"I... Would you..." Genny sighed, closed her eyes, and gulped. "Will you walk me down the aisle? I mean, I know you don't really—"

"And that, daughter, will be my pleasure."

Now Genny sniffled. "I'm... I want to call you, you know, father, but I'm not sure if..."

"When the time is right, I'll be Da, Genevieve." Padraic smiled and blotted at his own eyes.

It felt as if a weight were lifted from David's chest. One he hadn't even known existed. Because now Genny might get the family she deserved, instead of the one she'd only ever known and feared.

Strapped into their seats in the jet, Genevieve looked out one last time and there, on the other side of the barricade, stood her father. Padraic O'Shaunessy. A man she'd barely met but now knew as her father—or Da, he'd insisted.

"He's coming to visit in a couple of weeks," David reminded her.

"I know. Just… We're leaving him here alone to deal with the whole Marrer thing and Danu and Berith and…"

"He's older and stronger and a whole heap more able to deal with it than us, my love. Now wave goodbye and smile then turn around. We're going home and we've lots of plans to make. Among other things."

In the last twenty-four hours he'd made several cryptic remarks like that. So, she waved goodbye to Padraic through the small window then turned to David. "What do you mean by that?"

"Well, I read somewhere that children conceived in the air were easier to raise and better as first children." He grinned with a wicked glint in his eyes, while the thrum of engines increased and the jet moved onto the runway.

"David!" But even though his words were maybe a little scandalous, she couldn't help but grin. "That sounds—"

"Inventive? Ingenious? Amazing?"

"Oh, my Gods!" She reached out. "Well, I guess I'm game to try if you are. But I'd rather wait 'til after the wedding to, you know, be showing."

"Then we'd best plan for sooner rather than later, my love. I'm done waiting."

Epilogue

Turning away from the barricade, watching the jet taxiing down the runway, Padraic felt something inside him shifting. An unfamiliar sensation. Loneliness. One he'd hoped and prayed never to experience. At least, never again.

A shimmering started before him. One he knew well. Danu.

The figure of a woman in her thirties. Curvaceous and bubbly with bright green eyes and curly red hair. Her lips bee-stung and a deep rosy pink. She hadn't assumed this figure with him before, but that wasn't unusual. As a Goddess, she could take on any shape she wanted.

"Padraic. I finally tracked you down." There was a waspish bite to her voice.

"I was seeing my daughter and David off. They're going home." He hoped she'd understand it made him feel—he cast about for the right word to fit the emotion—incomplete.

"Ah. Oh yes. Child. Daughter. Of course. Now, I need you to do something for me. It's, shall we say, sensitive? I've been in contact with Berith." She made the words sound like a swear word, then winced and shuddered.

"Aye? Is that so?"

"Yes. Marrer is after a girl. The daughter of one of his demons." She shoved a photo into his hand. He didn't look at it, and instead focused on the woman before him.

"Why?"

She waved her hand in the air. "How am I supposed to know? But she's somehow important, and Berith thinks we need her to defeat Marrer. He wants us to bring Lucifer into the discussions. As if I want to see him again." Now she sniffed. "After the way he spoke to me last time? Honestly. The nerve of him. I'm a *Goddess*!"

Padraic knew not to laugh and curbed the reaction hard. "Once I have her, then what?"

"Oh, how the hell would I know? You'll have to ask Berith. He went on and on, but it was sooo boring!" Danu rolled her eyes. "Anyway, she's in Australia. You need to go get her. Immediately. So go on, trot off and do that, and I'm going home. I stink of sulfur now, and it'll take days to get rid of the smell."

The Goddess wheeled away, and he called out, "I'll be needing time off in a few weeks off. My daughter is marrying and—"

"Then you best get about your task quickly, hadn't you?" With that she dissolved into the air, and he huffed.

"Jaysus, Mary, and Joseph. She gets more demanding every day."

Padraic glanced down at the photo and felt shock wash over him. The woman in the image was perfection. Small, with red-golden hair. Beautiful with classically aligned features. Beside her stood another woman, tall though slightly built, with large glasses obscuring her face and a deep red blush. Her hair a curtain of burnished copper. He dismissed her as irrelevant. If he knew correctly, most people involved with paranormals had unnaturally perfect features. Otherworldly, some might say.

He sighed. "I need to talk to Berith," he murmured and reached into his pocket for his mobile phone and dialled.

"Yes?" The answer was delivered in harsh, scratchy tones.

"I need to talk to Ba'al Berith. It's Padraic O'Shaunessy." It was all he could say really. He knew no other facts, and he didn't think Berith would appreciate him telling some drone that he'd been given a mission by Danu that linked to him.

The sound of an indrawn breath filled the air. "I'll have him call you." Then the line disconnected.

Padraic stared at the phone in his hand. "Well, so much for that." He dropped the phone back into his pocket. He may as well go home and wait to be contacted then make plans.

The End
Maybe...

The Celtic Cupid Trilogy

When Cupid—otherwise known as Diocail— is banished from his home on a remote Scottish Island, he's set a series of tasks by the great god Lugh, who also happens to be his father.

In **Blame The Wine**, he must bring two lovers together... BBW Cara and James, the man she's lusted over from afar who happens to be a super geek and head Veha Industries.

In **A Stranger's Embrace**, Diocail is driven to help an

emotionally fragile Jane and Davis, a famous author. The task is more complicated, with the existence of Carstairs her could-be ex-husband and teenage daughter, Frannie.

In ***Revenge on Cupid***, Diocail must take the ultimate chance and find his own happily ever after with Simone. Sometimes the past gets in the way and HEA's don't come cheap though.

The dusty, dingy little diner was full, even with its current state of cleanliness—or lack thereof. People from the surrounding offices didn't care about anything except the incredible, well-prepared food at a reasonable cost. They flooded in, like waves to the shore. As one tide left, another swept in.

"Honestly, Simone. I'm going to try getting his attention one more time. If that doesn't work, I'm out of there. I mean, how long can I keep trying?" Cara picked at the caramel tart she hadn't been able to resist with the cheap metal fork and flicked the blob of fresh cream that sat on top to the side of the plate.

"You've said that tons of times before. Besides, what are you going to do to get his attention? Hmm? Walk naked through the typing pool?" Simone bobbed the straw in her smoothie as she eyed her friend with a frown. "It's been what? Eighteen months since you saw him, and you've mooned over him from a distance ever since you met him. You need to move on, Cara. That is, unless there's something you haven't shared?"

The query was arch. Cara shivered even as she shook her head. "No."

Simone quirked an eyebrow, obviously unconvinced with the answer. Cara let out a deep sigh of frustration. "There's a position...it's only temporary, for a PA reporting directly to him." She speared a forkful of tart, chewed quickly and swallowed, before continuing. "In his office, full-time for the period of the engagement. I saw the memo yesterday. I mean, I have the skills, right? I can type, answer phones, make coffee, file, greet people. What's more, I can probably do it better than all those size eights in the typing pool that Ms. Jackman seems to prefer." She nodded thoughtfully. "All I have to do is get past the ogre in Human Resources."

Simone stared at her, disbelief clear on her face. "Girl, I so remember that woman. If you think you can get past her, you're doing better than I ever did. That's why I left Veha Industries, remember? Maybe it's time to haul out your resumé and consider some other options. Look for something better." Simone shook her head and billows of her crimson hair swirled through the still air.

Cara understood Simone only had her best interests at heart. But this time she knew the outcome would be different. Hell, she could feel it in the air. The tingle of expectation.

"Cara, the HR ogre will hang you out for breakfast before she offers you anything like a position in that office. Remember her mantra? Good looks and good work make for a positive workplace!"

Simone didn't sugar-coat anything. It was another great reason for their long- term friendship. Honesty. But Cara didn't want to hear the truth in the statement. Even if it was exactly as her friend said.

Cara nodded quickly. "Yeah, I know, but if I don't try, then I won't know how close I can get to him, right? And the only way to catch his attention is to get past *her* and see him in person." Cara quaked a little at the information she needed to share. The favor she needed to ask. "Anyway, I tidied up my resumé and dropped the application into a memo envelope yesterday, so it's too late to back out now. I mean, fortune favors the brave. Doesn't it? If I don't snag an interview, I'm going to visit the career advisor across the street and register with them." She shrugged. "I'll look for temp work until something more long-term shows up. I can see what they have on offer and well...who knows? Maybe a job with the right boss is just waiting for me. But I'd rather this worked out, to be honest." Her voice trailed off into a whisper. "I really wish he would notice me."

Simone took a long slurp of her banana drink, and Cara noticed her questioning gaze even as she squirmed. Finally, Simone nodded.

"It's your funeral. So anyway, you'd better show me this memo if you want me to be a referee for you. I'm guessing that's what you need, right? I'll have to know what I'm supposed to say about you before they ring."

Cara smiled. "Thanks, Simone. I knew I could count on you." She slipped a piece of paper out of her handbag and handed it over. "Sorry it's a bit creased. It was in the bottom of my bag, I stashed it so none of the others from the pool would see. You know how it is."

Available from Love Books Publishing
books2read.com/CelticCupid

Direct Autographed Copy
https://www.imogenenix.net/CelticCupid

Star of Ishtar

Warriors of the Elector
Book One

The first time Elara laid eyes on Grayson was when he rescued her from the clutches of a madman and his scientists who were kidnapping humans and conducting horrific experiments on them. That was years ago. In spite of her attempts to deepen their relationship, they remained nothing more than close friends. Now Elara is a medic with the Admiralty, and she knows what she wants. It's been Grayson since the beginning. When Elara is stationed on the *Star of Ishtar*, she arrives with a plan to further her career. But this time her plan has an added bonus—to finally get her man.

Grayson's spent years fighting the connection between himself and Elara. He's certain it only exist because he saved her life. But his will is failing, and he fears he just might give in to temptation.

"I finally made it." Elara Sudonne watched as the hull of the *Star of Ishtar* loomed in the inky darkness. She clutched her hands tightly together as the shuttle approached the hulking battleship.

This would be her new home and first combat ST placement for the Earth Empire. She quaked inwardly with nerves but fought to keep her serene exterior. Previously her deployments had consisted solely of on-planet expeditions and in rehabilitation and dirtside facil-ities. When the chance had arisen to move to the battleship, she'd grabbed it with both hands.

The frigid air chilled her bones as she sat in her shuttle seat, but a trickle of sweat inched its way down her back under the fresh gray wool flight uniform. Little puffs of vapor escaped her mouth as she rubbed her arms. Nerves stretched tight, she looked through the small portal at the front of the vessel. She wanted to tug at the collar that somehow seemed to have grown tighter as the ship loomed ahead, but instead she firmed her mouth, straightened her spine, and concentrated on the future.

"So damned long." She'd been working toward this outcome since the day Grayson Myatt and Duvall McCord had saved her from her Ru'Edan captors. She was lucky, she'd survived the 'experimentation' of the Ru'Edan leader Crick Sur Banden's scientists. "And all I have to remind me are my scars." She didn't grin at her own joke.

The person seated behind her jostled but she ignored it, lost in her memories. On that day, so very long ago, the young Elara, fresh-faced and with idealistic views of the empire, was taken from the mall where she'd been shopping with friends, thrust into the back of a transport vehicle, and given to the Ru'Edan scientists to experiment on.

For days they'd worked on her and others, seeking an average pain threshold of humans, slicing her skin then noting reactions and how long it took to heal. They'd cut her arms, body, and even her face, and now she carried the extensive scarring of the exercise as a reminder to herself and others of what they were fighting for. Freedom. The freedom of Earth and its allied planets.

She'd never relinquished hope, it had been her constant companion as she fought against the all-consuming terror. Then they'd found her in that dirty, disused warehouse. They'd found others too, in various states of death and decay. The smells of despair had filled the air with a fetid ripeness that she'd never been able to forget.

Since that day she'd promised herself that she would pay the Ru'Edan back for what they'd done to her. What they'd taken from her. Over the years, she tempered and honed the rage while remaining adamant that she would see the final act played out. She couldn't physically fight, but she had learned about trauma, knew it and understood how it affected a person, and used it as a weapon.

The iron will forged through her experiences had fed her determination, and she'd applied herself to study, finishing in the top ten percent of her class. She entered the medical program at the academy, working hard to excel. Her family remained supportive if perplexed as to why she had chosen to keep reminding herself of what had happened.

The maw of the *Star of Ishtar* loomed closer, opening its cavernous mouth as she watched through the portal. She could hear the voices of the shuttle crew signaling their intention to enter and land, the tinny confirmation coming swiftly. She watched avidly while the shuttle maneuvered, imagining the invisible shields dropping to allow it entry.

Her hands twisted with fear and anger, but she tamped down her emotions. Anger never helped anyone. Staying strong, knowing your history, and ensuring it couldn't be repeated, they were the answers, she told herself firmly, pulling herself from the grip of a dark past so horrific she still saw it in her dreams. She pushed it away to the recesses of her mind and focused on what she was about to do.

A squark overhead, the usual mechanical sound that alerted all on board to a transmission by the captain, caught her attention. "Attention all passengers. We are entering the shuttle bay. Please ensure when you disembark you remove all personal items. Move beyond the white line and wait for your designation."

The lights of the bay flashed as they entered, and once again Elara marveled at how far humanity had moved since they had first walked the Earth. She saw the opening of the structure as the shuttle moved into the bay, inching forward slowly until it stopped its ponderous motion and began its descent to the floor. Something deep inside warmed even as the shuttle's environmental systems began to synchronize with the cooler temperature of the *Star of Ishtar*, and she felt a smile crawl its way over her face.

Elara breathed in deeply, inhaling the metallic-tasting, recycled air and welcoming the calmness that settled on her body. Her eyes closed as she filled her lungs. "I'm here." There was more than a little satisfaction in her tone, and she smiled. She slowly exhaled, finding that center of peace she relied on.

A loud thud and clank echoed as the deep drone split the air. The engines were powering down, and there she was, on one of the Earth Empire's Emeritus class battleships. She sat in her seat, waiting for the all clear from the captain, and once it sounded through the cabin, she rose, tugging at the webbing belt and disengaging it.

The small backpack beside her was all she carried as she made her way to the exit, not needing to duck as so many others did. She stepped through the door, her hands gripping the rail of the cold, metal stairs which connected to the side of the gray shuttle.

She clambered down them slowly, savoring the experience. The sting of the cold on her hands from the stairs, frigid from even their brief exposure to the blackness of space, made her flinch inwardly. The shuttle journey from the Admiralty's strategic base at Aenna to their current position had taken just over an hour, but the whole time it felt like her heart had been in her throat. Her mouth was dry as she followed the new recruits from the ship into the landing bay. She stopped, silently noting the slight mustiness of the air, the recycled quality easily recognizable. Everything, including the oxygen, needed recycling in space.

All around her people swarmed, either around the ships or into the dogleg line that now formed ahead of her. Someone had opened the baggage locker of the shuttle, and the sound of dropping bags hitting the plascrete floor echoed in the air. Another crewmember guided trolleys to the other side of the shuttle, pulling out boxes with important day-to-day items for the ship, including vaccines and plants. She watched briefly, all the while listening to the alien cacophony. Voices called in welcome to old crewmembers, while new ones watched, many goggle-eyed in the fresh uniforms of newly minted officers and crewmembers.

Her gaze flicked around quickly, taking in the sights, sounds, and smells, pungent with oils and grease; burning smells from the scorched plascrete and the press of sweaty or nervous bodies. She joined the line silently, tacking onto the end, and stayed at parade rest, knowing the welcoming voice would cut through the air soon enough. She felt somehow disconnected from the main throng. Perhaps the knowledge that this was the outcome she had worked for years to achieve set her apart. However, still, she felt so...distant from everything around her. She smiled secretly at the bout of whimsy.

"Attention!" The voice boomed out over the plascrete of the docking bay, and she snapped her body into position, noting the commander who had bellowed the words. Technically, she outranked most members aboard the *Star of Ishtar*, except for the command and leadership staff, but she knew all newcomers had to join the welcoming parade, regardless of rank.

Fleet Captain Elphin came into view, his tired features topped by salt-and-pepper gray hair, which highlighted his cool blue eyes. Elara also recognized a body prone to a little middle-aged thickness. Following behind him was his second-in-command, Duvall McCord. A young up-and-coming officer, his status as a fast-tracking officer heading toward his own command, with Elphin both his mentor and captain, had become almost legendary at the academy.

She looked closely at McCord, noting the dynamic drive of his actions and movements. Soon he would achieve a promotion to captain, and she rejoiced for her friend. She'd followed his career with interest and had to tamp down a smile as his eyes betrayed the shock of seeing her before settling into their flat command persona. So he hadn't been apprised of her deployment, she noted, and she had to restrain the tiny feeling of surprise and satisfaction. She filed that snippet of information away.

She caught sight of the man standing behind Duvall. Grayson Myatt. He'd made her heart beat faster for years. Tall and blond with a muscular build and a sexy, tight, little butt, he had pools of deep-blue eyes that had always made her think of forever. He had a growth of stubble on his chiseled jaw, and her fingers itched to touch his perfect lips. Yes, since the day he'd found her in that nasty warehouse tied down like a ragged animal, she'd worshipped him from afar.

Now she had her opportunity to tangle with him, hopefully much closer than any chance that had ever come her way before. With a sigh, she pulled her gaze back to the captain and forced herself to concentrate on his words. She couldn't afford to have her commanding officer angry due to her being distracted.

"Welcome to the *Star of Ishtar*. Most academy recruits want to join us because of what we represent, but on this ship, we only take the best of the best. So, if you made it here, you're the ones we wanted to take a look at. Getting here is only the first step. Staying here is harder to achieve. Our people are the best. Earn your place, and in return, we'll make you one of our crew—a member of the *Star of Ishtar*. Only the best and the brightest wear our uniform and badge. You'll be expected to perform to your absolute limit then give some more. We don't tolerate people who don't pull their weight. Do us proud and wear your uniform with pride." The captain looked out over the new members of his crew. His voice had echoed during his speech, and now it died away.

He scanned the faces before him, and she could almost read his thoughts. There were new security officers and a smattering of other crew. Some of them were young and impressionable, and she knew a few wouldn't make the cut as crewmembers. Others would carve out their place on the *Star of Ishtar* and move to better positions and placements, like she would: the new SurgiTech, a younger female, experienced but untried on board a ship. She smiled at that thought.

Some of those who stood with her would be replaced as they failed the exacting standards the captain set. She'd heard that he was a firm captain, fair but demanding. He'd have to be to command this ship. The Ishtar had well over five hundred at full capacity, and the captain could select their placements as his command staff saw fit from the many who applied to join the crew. She sensed his satisfaction with the choices in the relaxation of his body.

Abruptly, he turned to Duvall, breaking her study of him. "Get them to where they need to present themselves." His words echoed as he walked away. He had a purposeful stride. Quick but unhurried, like he knew where he was going and how to get there. A man who knew how to get what he wanted. Someone to respect and admire.

"My name is Commander Duvall McCord. I am your second-in-command, and my direct subordinate is Commander Grayson Myatt. While you are aboard the *Star of Ishtar* you will be required to fulfill your duties efficiently. As Captain Elphin said, do your job right and you will be one of ours, with all the benefits that come with being a crewmember of the *Star of Ishtar*."

He paused and eyeballed each of the newer recruits, those fresh from the academy. Many of them paled under his gaze, and she smiled inwardly. Even the older people in the line seemed to quake beneath his scowl. He'd always had that air of innate authority, even when barely out of the academy himself. She knew his methods and watched him make full use of the carefully practiced tone of presence.

"Each of you has been assigned. You will present yourselves to the chief of your section. Those details will be found in your orders. Commander Myatt has organized a team to escort you to your cabins. You will have approximately one hour to prepare. We've arranged for crewmembers to escort you to your superiors. Be ready to present for duty. Any issues, you will, of course, take up with your section commander. Should there be need to take any further action, you will see Commander Myatt. You should only see me if you are a command crewmember or as a point of discipline. I am not one for small talk, so if you present to me, have a very good reason."

He delivered the words slowly and deliberately, and Elara restrained a small smile on hearing at least one gulp from those in the line nearest her.

"We run a tight ship here. Discipline and commitment are the two key factors we look for beyond loyalty in our crew. You will from henceforth represent our ship everywhere, and we do not tolerate anything less than the best." He looked around once more, the stern demeanor he wore so well reinforcing the message. If she hadn't known him for so long, she too might have missed the hint of humor glinting in his eyes, the one many took for coldness.

Her legs ached, and she wanted to move and relieve the pressure on them, but she held herself still, waiting for the command to dismiss. She wouldn't let herself or him down now. Not after she'd worked so long to achieve this position.

As the new ST, she had no previous experience on ships. She had vast experience in the field, but Elara was aware that would count for little in the eyes of most of the crew. She didn't intend to signal a weakness to anyone and least of all on her first day aboard the *Star of Ishtar*. That thought held her still and controlled.

She had big shoes to fill after her predecessor, Jamieson, had retired, even though she knew she could fill the void he'd left behind. As a long-term member of the crew—over twenty years—his tenure on the *Star of Ishtar* had placed him aboard since its launch. Due to his experience in the heat of battle with the Ru'Edan he had made a name for himself as the coldest of cold in the hottest of situations. She hoped to emulate that herself and carve out her own place aboard the Ishtar, as its crew lovingly knew her.

Duvall and Grayson knew how much she wanted to prove herself. They just wouldn't have expected it here, on the Ishtar.

She watched Duvall study her, then, quickly turning on his heel, call to those assembled, "Dismissed."

Once they started to move away, she softened her stance, preparing to turn when the call came.

"Sudonne! A moment if you please."

Elara turned to face Duvall. "Commander?"

"Welcome to the *Star of Ishtar*, Elara. While I am surprised you're the new ST, Grayson and I are pleased you could join us. But how did you manage to pull it off? Keeping it quiet that you were the new ST?" he asked, his voice deep enough to make most women shiver with anticipation.

She smiled, thinking it was a shame she didn't have any feelings for him except sisterly attachment, but then again, given his lack of deep commitment to women, maybe it wasn't such a shame after all.

She understood what drove him. He wanted his own ship and to captain his own future. They'd spent many nights over wine or ale discussing his beliefs that commitment grounded a person. Inwardly, she shrugged. He'd make those calls for himself, though she was sure that one day he would come across someone who would make him consider his choices a little more thoroughly.

"I'm pleased to be here, Duvall. Having an uncle who happens to be an admiral, he was able to let Captain Elphin know that I wanted to surprise you. It's a small world in the Admiralty. Elphin already knew of me, so he okayed my placement. Once the powers knew there was no impediments to me joining the crew, it was fairly simple from there." She felt a small smile creep onto her face, then let it drop away. "What do you think Grayson thinks?"

"Ah, still chasing him, are you?" He grinned, his eyes twinkling. "I think he'll be pleased you're finally old enough and you're here." He looked her straight in the eye. "But you may just need to remind him of that particular fact." He motioned for her to go before him, barking out a deep laugh. "Come on, I'll show you to your cabin."

Available from Love Books Publishing
Available in Ebook via Books2Read

Direct Autographed Copy
https://www.imogenenix.net/Warriors1

The Blood Bride by Imogene Nix

Hope just wants to be an ordinary nestling. She went to college and escaped, but now she's back and there's a secret everyone is keeping from her.

Xavier is the new master of the nest, ready to welcome home the daughter of the house who he has never met. He's unprepared for the woman who steals his breath and enchants him.

Now Hope and Xavier must fight for lives and those of the innocents. After all, it is only by overcoming the rogues that they will have a chance of a timeless future together. But will it be in time?

PROLOGUE

As silence descended on the house, the shadows grew—dark grays and blacks that bled into each other. First one figure then another broke away, making a run toward the house. Silent as the grave, they moved swiftly over dew-slicked grass. Then they stopped still. Waiting. Not a movement betrayed them until a signal propelled them back into action and they started crawling upwards. The walls damp coating no barrier to the intruders that ascended in the darkness.

The sound of each window breaking shattered the quiet—the figures were inside. Screams echoed through the night. Yet, in this area of large estates, heavy with noise-absorbing shrubbery, no one could hear those within. The blood-curdling screams went on and on before finally dying away.

Just one sound echoed through the night: The sobbing of a child.

The front door opened and figures trooped out—ghostly specters against an inky night sky, broken by a single outline. A child in white, carried at the center of the pack.

No sound broke the silence as they moved toward the trees surrounded the house.

Flames now licked at the manor: A deathly glow of oily smoke rising.

All that remained was a single person—wrapped in a cape of midnight blue beyond the house—watching them melt away.

Jemima moved toward the burning structure, breaking into a run as she breached the threshold. Vainly she attempted to enter, but the heat drove her back.

Now dashing tears from her face, she raced across the graveled driveway toward the gates, where the guardhouse was located. No sign of life existed within the building and some instinct of survival slowed her pace to a careful creep. Out of breath and heaving from exertion, she nervously checked within.

Small puffs of white vapor colored the glass. She darted from one window to another. Her cloak drawn tightly around her body, hoping it would camouflage her from sight.

Satisfied, Jemima entered through the heavy, wooden front door and moved toward the phone she spied on the floor. Her eyes darting here and there she dialed, listening to the rotary motor as it returned to the proper position. Time was short and if *they* came back, she needed to have shared the message.

The phone rang once. Twice. With a brrping sound it connected.

"Hello?" A male answered and she felt a warm flush of relief at the voice. A voice she knew well.

"The manor has been breached. The girl child taken." The words erupted and her hand trembled.

"On our way." The click of the receiver being replaced echoed loudly in the stillness of the room.

Copper. She smelled copper.

Her stomach soured, knowing it meant more deaths. Jemima looked around for the gun—a gun with deadly, holy water-infused copper bullets—she knew was hidden somewhere in the room. A gun she couldn't find. *No divine intervention exists here*, she thought.

Hopefully *they* didn't remain. Feeding. If they were still here, that's what they would be doing. She found a corner and scrunched down, hiding from sight.

Crouched low, she tried to stay as still as possible, listening for sounds of the vehicles she knew would be coming. She dug her fingers into the flesh of her arms; remaining aware enough to stop before drawing blood. That would surely bring them out. Jemima dragged the cloak around her to capture the warmth, yet there was little to be found.

The sounds of engines roused her from the corner of the room.

Jemima inched toward the window, the lead of the old glass distorting her view, hearing raised voices she knew Mistress Cressida had arrived.

Jemima retreated. Remained hidden from the woman because if she knew, all may well be lost. From the shadowed room she listened to the conversation...

"It smells like Estersham." The Mistress' eyes closed. "If it is, we have a problem." She turned once more, her face set and eyes now glacial in intensity. "James?"

The man nodded as if he knew what was to come.

"If I take those steps, I cannot return. Another must stand in my place." Her voice hardened while her eyes glittered in the dim light, piercing in their intensity.

Then the Mistress' voice called out in the near silence. "You and yours have been my loyal servants for so many years. I took an oath to protect you long ago. I renewed it with marriage and births, over and over. Now, my home and yours have been breached and this child taken from us. The girl child, who will be the hope and salvation of our kind, was ripped from the bosom of our nest. I will repay your loyalty and I will get her back." The words of power rippled in the night and licked at Jemima's skin.

Available in Ebook
books2read.com/BloodBride-Nix

Direct Autographed Copy
https://www.imogenenix.net/BloodBride

Also by Imogene Nix

<u>Warriors of the Elector</u>

- Star of Ishtar
- Starline
- Starfire
- Star of the Fleet
- Starburst
- The Star of Eternity

The Star of Ishtar & Starline - Print

Starfire & Star of the Fleet - Print

Starburst & The Star of Eternity - Print

<u>Blood Secrets</u>

- The Blood Bride
- The Illuminated Witch
- The Sorcerer's Touch

<u>The Secrets World:</u>

<u>Blood Secrets</u>

- The Blood Bride
- The Illuminated Witch
- The Sorcerer's Touch

<u>House Secrets</u>

- As Dawn Breaks

- Immortal Consequences
- Unnamed Book III

All That Glitters - a House Secrets Novella

Danu's Secrets

- The Downfall of Padraic O'Shaunessy
- Unnamed Secrets Book II

The Automaton Series

- Haven House
- Nobel Crest

The Search Duology

- Miss Elspeth's Desire
- Miss Isabelle's Craving

Duology World Novels

- A Very Merry Widow (coming soon)

Reunion Trilogy

- War's End
- The Assassin
- Executing Justice

The Reunion Trilogy in Paperback

Sex Love & Aliens

- Tangled Webs

- False Webs
- Covert Webs

21st Testing Protocol

- Cyborg: Redux
- Children Of A Greater Evil
- When Evil Came To Stay
- Finis: The War To End All Wars

Celtic Cupid Trilogy

- Blame The Wine
- A Stranger's Embrace
- Revenge On Cupid

The Celtic Cupid Trilogy in Paperback

Zombieology

- The Reset
- I Dream of Zombies
- The Six Million Dollar Zombie
- Make Room For Zombies
- Days of Our Zombies
- Unnamed Zombiology title (coming soon)

Knights of Pleasure

- Silken Knights

Single Titles

The Chocolate Affair (also in Print)

Falling In Love Again (Previously A Sapphire For Karina)

BioCybe (also in Print)

Hesparia's Tears (also in Print)

Tomorrow's Promise

A Bar In Paris (also in Print)

Inheritance Of The Blood (also in Print)

The Plan

Loving Memories (also in Print)

Hero of Heartbreak Hill (also in Print)

My One & Only

Curse Bound

Raspberry Dreams (Not Yet Released)

Non Fiction

Self Publishing: Absolute Beginners Guide (With Suzi Love)

Written as Ciara Cave

25 Curated Ways To Get Rid Of Telemarketers

Book Signings for Absolute Beginners

About the Author

Imogene is published in a range of romance genres including Paranormal, Science Fiction and Contemporary. She is mainly published in the UK and USA.

In 2010, Imogene Nix (the pen name not Imogene herself) was born. Imogene sat down and worked tirelessly for 3 months culminating in the book Starline, which became the first in a trilogy titled, "Warriors of the Elector." Since then she's had over 30 titles published and is now focusing on hybridising herself - with a mixture of traditionally published and self-published works.

In fact, she's taking control of many of her back catalogue books, which are slowly re-releasing as self-published titles.

Imogene is a member of a range of professional organisations world wide, and believes in the mantra of mentoring and paying it forward and is actively involved in mentorship (through NaNoW-rimo and her vlog: In The Chair With Imogene Nix) and tutoring of new and upcoming authors.

In her spare time she loves to drink coffee, wine & eat chocolate and is parenting her spoiled dog and a ferocious cat along with her husband and daughter and looks forward to weekends away with her husband in their caravan "The Seven Year Hitch!" Do look forward to her caravan romance at some point!

To Contact Imogene

www.imogenenix.net
imogene@imogenenix.net

Sign up for her newsletter at
https://www.imogenenix.net/Signup

 facebook.com/ImogeneNix

twitter.com/ImogeneNix

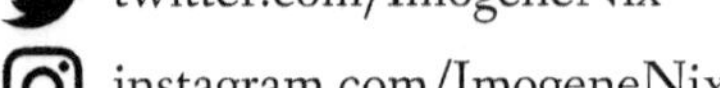 instagram.com/ImogeneNix

bookbub.com/authors/imogenenix

www.ingramcontent.com/pod-product-compliance
Lightning Source LLC
Chambersburg PA
CBHW071020180726
48291CB00004B/1549